Thunder!

Momentarily, she lost her grip on the wheel, so sudden and sharp was the explosion.

She heard MacDougall shouting, "Hold to the left . . . keep bearing left . . . that's it . . . brakes, Laura, brakes!"

She felt the truck shudder to a halt. Relief left her weak and drained, and she almost fell out of the cab into MacDougall's arms.

"You did it! Laura, you did it!"

Suddenly the mud, the rain and the storm were all forgotten. MacDougall was holding her in his arms. When his mouth crushed hers and his body pressed her hard against the side of the truck, she could feel nothing but the alarming response of her own passion. . . .

FRANCES LLOYD
resides in Victoria, Australia. She has traveled throughout Australia and Europe, and her love for the outback is vividly reflected in all her work, which includes an Australian travel guide. This is her first Silhouette Romance.

Dear Reader:

I'd like to take this opportunity to thank you for all your support and encouragement of Silhouette Romances.

Many of you write in regularly, telling us what you like best about Silhouette, which authors are your favorites. This is a tremendous help to us as we strive to publish the best contemporary romances possible.

All the romances from Silhouette Books are for you, so enjoy this book and the many stories to come. I hope you'll continue to share your thoughts with us, and invite you to write to us at the address below:

Karen Solem
Editor-in-Chief
Silhouette Books
P.O. Box 769
New York, N.Y. 10019

FRANCES LLOYD
Savage Moon

Silhouette *Romance*

Published by Silhouette Books New York

America's Publisher of Contemporary Romance

SILHOUETTE BOOKS, a Simon & Schuster Division of
GULF & WESTERN CORPORATION
1230 Avenue of the Americas, New York, N.Y. 10020

ISBN: 0-671-57200-8

First Silhouette Books printing January, 1983

10 9 8 7 6 5 4 3 2 1

Map by Ray Lundgren

America's Publisher of Contemporary Romance

Printed in the U.S.A.

Savage
Moon

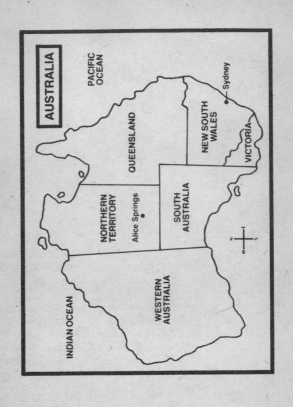

AUSTRALIA

PACIFIC OCEAN

QUEENSLAND

NEW SOUTH WALES

Sydney

VICTORIA

NORTHERN TERRITORY

Alice Springs

SOUTH AUSTRALIA

WESTERN AUSTRALIA

INDIAN OCEAN

N
W   E
S

Chapter One

It was the middle of the night when Laura stepped off the long-distance bus into the dusty road, her small suitcase in one hand, MacDougall's parcel in the other.

"Cheerio," called the bus driver. "Good luck!"

A few pale, curious faces peered sleepily through the dark anti-glare glass of the bus windows, faintly annoyed at being disturbed from their uncomfortable slumbers.

"Cheerio," echoed Laura, setting her suitcase down, reluctant now to let the bus go and leave her in this coal-hole darkness without a light glimmering anywhere. "Where did you say the hotel was?" she asked.

"Right opposite," said the bus driver, jerking his thumb toward the other side of the street. "Sure you'll be okay?" Suddenly he sounded anxious about her, all alone.

For a moment she would have given anything to have him jump down and escort her into the hotel, but pride made her assert her independence.

"Yes, I'll be fine," she said, trying not to let her voice waver. "They're expecting me."

"That's all right then," said the driver. "You'll be okay.

Old Ma Burdekin's a good sort. She'll look after you. You won't forget to hand over the package to MacDougall, will you?" He seemed a little dubious now he had entrusted it to her.

When he had learned that Laura was to alight at Camel Creek, he had asked her if she would mind delivering the truck part he had brought up for a man named MacDougall, who would call at the Camel Creek Hotel for it the next day.

"I'll do it first thing in the morning," Laura promised.

"Okay, thanks," said the driver, and once again, "cheerio."

The doors closed with a slow hiss and the bus moved off, stirring the dust around Laura's feet. As its taillights disappeared in the distance, she watched with a feeling of emptiness even greater than that which had filled her recently. In the first moments after the brightness of the bus had passed, the darkness closed around her like an enveloping cloak, and the feeling of being stranded in space without a lifeline was acute.

As her eyes grew accustomed to the dark, she realized that there was more light than she had thought. She looked up. The sky was a cobweb of frosty jewels spun from horizon to horizon, with the Milky Way so thick with stars it was like a sparkling waterfall. In the silent main street of the deserted town, a handful of buildings loomed ghostly and forbidding, and there wasn't a light anywhere, save for the stars.

It was cold, and Laura clutched her thick cardigan around her, tying the belt tighter. She picked up her suitcase and looked across the wide empty street at the hotel. It was a double-story building with a rickety wooden balcony running around the two sides she could see. Over the entrance its name was set boldly in plaster. It was just discernible in the starlight—CAMEL CREEK HOTEL 1893. Laura crossed the street. As she stood uncertainly outside the hotel, the sound of loud and resonant snoring drifted down from the balcony above.

A gravelly male voice rasped rudely and sleepily, "Pack it in, mate!" He presumably gave the offender a shove because there was a snort and a groan and then silence.

Laura flinched. What on earth was she doing in a place like this? She must have been mad to come. She wondered what she was expected to do. The hotel knew she would be arriving on the bus but it seemed that no one had aroused themselves to greet her, or perhaps Mrs. Burdekin had forgotten. For one moment she contemplated calling out to whoever was sleeping on the upstairs veranda, then decided against such a move since it was bound to make her unpopular.

Instead, she approached the front door and looked for a night bell. Peering and probing in the gloom, she did not find a bell, but all at once noticed a small piece of card stuck between the door and the jamb. Hoping it was a message for her, she fumbled in her handbag for her key ring, which had a tiny flashlight attached, and by its light managed to decipher the writing.

"Miss Fairchild," said the hasty scribble, and Laura was immediately relieved to find she had not been forgotten, *"your room is up the backstairs, Number 13."*

That was all. She stared at it. What a welcome! Had there been anywhere else to go she would have run from this seedy place in disgust, but there was nowhere else. Camel Creek boasted only one hotel and this was it. With a sigh, she picked up her suitcase once more and made her way around to the back of the hotel where she hoped to find the stairs referred to in the note.

It was not easy in the dark, and she stumbled a few times over unseen obstacles, once kicking a trash can so loudly that the sound seemed to reverberate throughout the whole universe. She half-expected cries of outrage from the upstairs veranda, but none came and silence settled once more.

At last she found the stairs, half concealed under a canopy of rampant creeper. Still there was no glimmer of light to show her the way so she plunged forward only to jump back quickly as something soft hit her in the face, and cobwebs clung stickily to her nose and cheeks. She gulped. It had felt like a rather large spider. Where was it now? Her skin prickled. She hated spiders. What else lurked on the staircase?

In some trepidation, she crept up the creaking wooden

9

stairs until she found herself at one corner of the balcony, which she now discovered ran right around the hotel. Dimly, she could see a couple of lumpy beds at one end, presumably occupied. There did not seem to be any more doors in that direction, only windows, so she tiptoed, as quietly as the old floorboards would allow, in the other. Eventually she came to a door which stood open. She plunged through into what at first seemed another tunnel of darkness, until she saw the glimmer of a weak light bulb just ahead. Underneath it she found a door with number 13 on it and breathed a sigh of relief. Just as well she wasn't superstitious, she thought wryly. It was hardly an auspicious start.

The door handle turned easily. It was some moments, however, before she found the light switch on the wall and flicked it on. A bulb, hiding under a pink plastic shade dangling from a cord looped over a hook above the end of the bed, shed light as dim as the one in the passage. In the center of the high ceiling was an old-fashioned punkah fan.

Laura looked around with distaste. An iron bed dominated the cell-like room. Beside it was an old-fashioned washstand with a square mirror, rather pitted. In another corner a wardrobe with peeling varnish also sported a mirror. Laura caught a glimpse of herself in it and was appalled at her gaunt and disheveled appearance.

Suddenly she felt desperately tired. The long bus journey and her fever of expectation, on top of everything else, had strained her resources to the limit. She flung the faded folk-weave counterpane and found, rather to her surprise, a neatly made bed, with pillowcase and sheets that, even in the ghastly light, were patently snow white and spotlessly clean.

Not wanting to create any further disturbance to the sleeping hotel by searching for one, she decided she could do without the bathroom until morning. She swiftly undressed, slipped into the nightdress she had fortunately packed right on top of her suitcase and climbed into bed. The sheets were chill and the bedsprings creaked, but she was too exhausted to care. In seconds she was in a deep sleep dreaming of her reunion with Eric. That he might no longer be at Camel Creek she had not even considered, even though it was nearly a year since she had heard from him, and then only a birthday card. Even though she was grown up, Eric never forgot her birthday.

Laura's one thought was to see him again. It was this thought that had dragged her through the recent painful weeks since her mother had been killed in a car crash. Eric, her half-brother, was all she had left now, and every day that passed the need to see him grew. It had begun the day she had sat down to write to him with the news of Lady Fairchild's death. Suddenly she had screwed up the sheet of writing paper and had tossed it into the wastepaper basket, possessed of an impulsive desire not to write but to go herself. Suddenly there had seemed to be nothing she wanted more in the world than to talk to Eric. He was many years older than she, and Laura had always admired him and felt a great affection for him, even though she had seen him seldom.

After her mother's death she had felt totally bereft, not because they had been close—Lady Fairchild had never really had much time for the daughter whose birth she had not welcomed; and she had never allowed motherhood to disrupt her considerable social life—but because suddenly she was all alone. Her mother's family had scarcely acknowledged her existence since they had not approved of the marriage, and on her father's side there were no close relatives except Eric.

Perhaps Laura would not have felt so lonely if her romance with Romilly Grant had not ended rather abruptly quite soon after her mother's death. No sooner was it known that Lady Fairchild had died leaving barely enough money to cover her debts than Romilly's interest in Laura had rapidly cooled. Although nothing was actually said, when Laura spotted his picture in a gossip column only two weeks after the funeral, with the daughter of a property tycoon, she knew it was all over.

With this realization, life had suddenly seemed just an enormous vacuum, and she had become moody and restless, and desperate for something or someone to cling to. So, when she had started to write to Eric, she had impulsively changed her mind. As soon as she was able she had taken indefinite leave from her job as a beauty consultant in an exclusive West

End salon in London. Before she could think of reasons why she should not go, she was on a flight to Australia.

When Laura woke on the morning after her arrival at Camel Creek, it was with a feeling of unreality. Was she really here in this dingy, down-at-heel Outback hotel and not in the tastefully decorated Kensington flat? Or was it all a dream?

The clumping of boots on the linoleum outside her bedroom door was no dream. They went to and fro several times until she decided that it was undoubtedly morning traffic to the bathroom. When there had been silence for some minutes she slipped out of bed, put on her dressing gown and scuffs and peered out of the door along the gloomy passage.

At the same moment a man emerged from a door at the far end, wearing only a towel around his waist, in spite of the chilly morning. Laura stared at him, and he stared at her, both somewhat surprised.

He was youngish, thirty or so, with damp tousled hair that was probably the color of wheat stubble when dry. It clung in curling tendrils on his forehead and there was a small nest of similarly colored hairs on his broad suntanned chest. She could not help noticing his broad shoulders and muscular forearms, which contrasted pointedly with slim hips only cursorily covered by the towel that barely reached his navel. His feet were in leather thong sandals.

Laura surprised herself by mentally comparing him with Romilly, who, at best, could only be called skinny, and who never managed to gain a respectable suntan. As she stared rather rudely at the man, the extraordinary notion swept through her head that to be held in this man's arms would put every other embrace she had ever experienced to shame.

She was so intent on her appraisal of him that she was, for a moment, unaware that he was equally as preoccupied surveying her. His eyes were as gray blue as the misty hills she had seen in the distance yesterday from the bus, and they traveled a slow sensuous route from her head to her toes, making her feel even more disconcerted. His was a searing look, an unmistakably male appraisal, but also, unnervingly, a look tinged with contempt. Laura was more stunned by this realization than anything. He was looking at her as though he loathed her. She felt enraged, insulted, and the smile she had been about to bestow on him, the polite greeting she had been about to utter, died on her lips.

Her cheeks burning with confusion, she withdrew and shut the door with a hasty slam. She heard the faint *flip-flop* of his sandals disappearing down the linoleum-covered passage. To her dismay she found she was shaking all over, even though she was not really cold. Grabbing the towel which was folded over the end of the bed, and her toilet bag, she decided to take advantage of the bathroom being unoccupied while she had the chance.

In daylight, the hotel, although obviously run down, did not look as seedy as it had last night. It was shabby but clean, and the water was hot in the shower. Laura allowed herself a few moments of blissful luxury as she let the steaming hot water cascade down over her shapely body, revitalizing her after the tiring travel of the past few days.

She smiled to herself, remembering how she had tiptoed up the backstairs in the middle of the night, petrified of encountering more spiders, or worse. But how much more horrified and outraged her fastidious mother would have been! The thought of her mother was sobering. She wished she felt more grief for the beautiful but frivolous and extravagant woman who had married her distinguished father, Sir Anthony Fairchild, the well-known anthropologist and writer. His first wife had died suddenly not long after his retirement from fieldwork, and as it was the first time they had been able to look forward to unlimited time together, he had been heartbroken.

Laura often wished she had known Eric's mother. She had felt guilty sometimes because she cherished a fondness for the gentle serene-faced woman she knew only from photographs that was somehow more real than the exasperated affection she had felt for her own mother.

Lillian Taft, debutante and social butterfly, had capitvated the grieving Sir Anthony and had swept him off his feet. However, by the time she was ten, Laura had known that their marriage was a mistake and that her father was not a happy man. His wife's increasingly selfish and extravagant ways saddened him, but, even then, still to some extent under her spell, he could deny her nothing. It was no wonder that his son, also an anthropologist, had slid unobtrusively off the scene and spent most of his life chasing after lost tribes or studying the vanishing cultures of this country or that. On the rare occasions he had returned to England and Turnwood Down, deep in greenbelt Surrey, he had enchanted a small girl with his tales of exotic places, terrifying her with masks and weapons he brought home from primitive tribes, but nevertheless making bright interludes in her rather lonely life.

After their father died, Eric did not come home again. Laura was almost grown-up then. When she left school, without any clear idea of what she wanted to do, she had let her mother decide for her, and consequently, through a friend of her mother's, had trained as a beautician.

"You've got most of my looks fortunately," declared her never-modest mother, "which is an advantage, I suppose, for a beauty consultant."

Laura had never shared her mother's conceit, however. She had often looked in the mirror and tried to see beauty in the pale skin, the large widely spaced, rather solemn greeny-brown eyes and prominent cheekbones, the straight dark hair and well-defined eyebrows, but had seen no more than a very ordinary girl with only a faint resemblance to the beauty her mother had been, and then still was. That was because she never saw her own eyes light up with happiness, flash with sudden anger at injustice, or her chin lift stubbornly when she was sure she was right, her mouth quiver appealingly when she was hurt. Laura's face was a kaleidoscope of expressions which in a dozen different ways made her more than beautiful—intriguing, some would have said.

Back in her hotel bedroom, she surveyed the new Laura in the cracked mirror, which thankfully returned her a less ghastly reflection than last night. She tugged at her now short-cropped hair, with only a passing regret for the luxurious locks she had kept from childhood. For ease of traveling, she had recklessly gone to a hairdresser and demanded to be shorn. Now she had the look of an impish sprite. The short boyish cut, with its full fringe and flicked-up ends on her cheeks, made her cheekbones more prominent, her eyes more expressive, but instead of twenty-two years old she looked more like fifteen. Carefully she made up her face to suit the new hairstyle, using eye shadow, mascara, foundation and lipstick, a touch of blusher, with the skill that was her profession. She had just wriggled into a pair of well-cut, well-fitted sky-blue slacks and a blue and white checked cotton shirt, when there was a tap at the door.

"Come in!" Laura called automatically.

She looked up and a dumpy little woman with gray hair screwed into a neat bun entered carrying a cup of tea. Her eyebrows rose slightly at the sight of the sleekly groomed girl.

"'Morning," she greeted Laura cheerfully. "I'm Mrs. Burdekin."

Laura flashed her a smile. "Oh . . . hello . . ."

"I see you settled yourself in all right last night," said the woman in a slow drawl. She looked Laura up and down curiously. "Brought you a cuppa, dear."

"Oh . . . thank you," said Laura, promptly, taking the proffered cup of tea. "Thank you very much."

"Sorry I wasn't about to let you in," apologized Mrs. Burdekin, "but I had to rush off to my sister's place in a hurry last night. She was taken ill suddenly. She lives a fair way out, so I stopped over. I hope you didn't mind finding your own way around."

"No, not at all," said Laura, glad of the hot tea. She added, "I'm sorry about your sister. I hope she's all right."

"Turned out to be appendicitis," said Mrs. Burdekin. "We called the Flying Doctor and they took her to hospital in the Alice." She saw Laura's puzzlement and added, "Alice Springs." Then she went on, "You wouldn't be a relative of Professor Fairchild's, would you, by any chance?"

Laura started. So she knew Eric. "Yes," she answered eagerly. "He's my brother. That's why I'm here. Can you show me where he lives?" Suddenly her heart was pounding with excitement again. However, it quickly turned to disappointment as Mrs. Burdekin shook her head.

"He doesn't live in Camel Creek now."

"He's gone. . . ." For the first time Laura realized what a fool she was to have come here without checking first. Eric could be anywhere—she knew that. "Do you know where he is now?" she asked hopefully.

Mrs. Burdekin said, "He left some of his things here. He's been off living with the aborigines for some months now. I don't know where exactly but MacDougall'll know." She glanced at Laura doubtfully. "Does he know you're coming?"

Laura shook her head. "No . . . you see, I . . ." Suddenly she was blurting out the whole story while Mrs. Burdekin listened, nodding sympathetically.

"Well, you'd better have a word with MacDougall, I reckon," she said at last. "He goes out with supplies once a month—he does the mail run to a few outlying stations and camps. He should've left last week but his truck broke down, and he had to send south for a part—"

"Goodness, yes!" cried Laura, remembering. "I've got it!"

"You've got it!" exclaimed the hotel proprietress. "How did you come by it? The bus was supposed to leave it around the back by the kitchen door. It wasn't there so I told Mac it couldn't have come. He's in a rare old mood about it now!"

Laura gulped. "I'm sorry. The bus driver gave it to me and said would I mind delivering it to him." She added, "I'd better do it right away. Where can I find him, Mrs. Burdekin?"

"He might still be in the dining room having his breakfast," said Mrs. Burdekin. "If not, he'll be over at Fogarty's Garage."

She left Laura to finish dressing. A few moments later Laura picked up her handbag, the truck part and the cup and saucer and started down the stairs she had noticed near the bathroom. They brought her down into the reception area and face to face with a sign saying DINING ROOM. She entered. There were three men there, one sitting alone, two at another table.

Hesitantly, she asked, "Is Mr. MacDougall here?"

Three pairs of eyes lifted and the men looked her over with smiling approval. One whistled low.

"Hey, look what the bus brought up," murmured one.

16

The oldest of the three said, "Mac's gone, sweetheart. What'd you want him for?"

"I . . . I have something for him," said Laura, a little embarrassed by their stares.

"Half 'is luck!" said one of the men. "Trust Mac. He has all the flamin' luck! Sure you haven't got something for me, love?"

Laura blushed at the tone of his remark and was glad when a waitress bustled in with a plate of bacon and eggs for one of the men. She turned to Laura. "Now what would you like, dear?" Taking the cup and saucer from Laura's hand, she ushered her to a table, brushing the crumbs off the tablecloth and straightening the cutlery and the vase of plastic flowers.

"I was looking for Mr. MacDougall," said Laura anxiously.

"He's gone," said the waitress.

Mrs. Burdekin came into the room and crossed to Laura. "MacDougall's gone, has he?" She looked around. "Oh, well, one of these lads can take the part over to him. Dave . . . ?" She beckoned to one of them.

Laura said hastily, "I . . . I'd rather take it myself. I want to talk to him . . . about my brother." She added, "I don't want to miss him."

Mrs. Burdekin glanced at the clock. "Well, don't be long, dear. We've nearly finished serving breakfast."

"It doesn't matter . . . I don't want any breakfast," said Laura hurriedly.

Mrs. Burdekin patted her shoulder. "You come back and have something to eat, and no arguing."

She and the waitress bustled off to the kitchen and as Laura left, one of the men called after her, "Watch out for MacDougall, love. He eats little girls for breakfast!"

Laura smiled weakly. Who was this MacDougall? He sounded formidable, and evidently he commanded considerable respect.

Outside the hotel Laura paused for a moment. Even though it was early morning, the glare hurt her eyes. The town was even smaller than she had realized and consisted of little more than the hotel, a garage, a couple of stores and a scattering of houses. There was scarcely a tree to be seen and

17

those that struggled for survival in the dusty red earth were bent and gnarled and as dried up as the earth around them. The landscape was flat in all directions with just a smudge of hills on the horizon. There was no sign of any creek, at least not with water in it; neither, Laura mused wryly, was there any sign of camels.

The sun was rapidly dissipating the early morning chill and as Laura moved out of the shadow of the hotel, still wearing her thick cardigan, she began to feel its warmth. Narrowing her eyes against the glare, she tripped lightly on sandaled feet through the red dust to the garage. It appeared to be deserted. Laura picked her way between the pools of oil and went up to the glassed-in office. She peered through the dusty window. There was no one there and the door was locked.

She called out, "Anyone around?"

There was no answer.

She wandered around but saw no sign of anyone. Then she heard the sound of metal striking metal, coming from the rear of the garage, so went to investigate. There she saw a number of vehicles, mostly lacking wheels or hoods or other vital parts, or in some cases they were just rusted shells. A man in blue overalls was bending over the engine of a truck. As Laura approached, a large dog sprang out from the shadows beneath the truck and took up a menacing stance facing her. He was huge, the size of a Great Dane but with the build of a greyhound, and the creamy color of a Labrador. He began to bark.

Laura stood stock-still, terrified. The man straightened up and looked around. "That'll do, Caesar!" The dog immediately stopped barking.

"G . . . good morning . . ." Laura started to say, and then gaped. It was the blond giant from the Camel Creek Hotel. He faced her, spattered with grease, nonsmiling.

"Jack's not around," he told her brusquely. "You'd better come back later." His eyes raked her in the same unnerving way as before, and she felt the same hot and cold shivering sensation as then.

"I was looking for Mr. MacDougall," she said. "Do you happen to know where I might find him?"

18

He strode toward her, stood looking down at her. "I am MacDougall," he said, his voice low, resonant and antagonistic.

Laura was taken aback. Somehow she had not expected this, and it threw her into quite unnecessary confusion.

She held out the package. "I believe this is the part you've been waiting for."

He snatched it from her. His eyes blazed. "What in the name of heaven are you doing with it?" He looked at her as though he thought she had stolen it.

"The bus driver asked me to give it to you," she explained, feeling ruffled by his unnecessarily sharp tone.

"Then why the hell didn't you?" he snapped. "I've been waiting a fortnight for this."

She bridled. "I've hardly had a chance. I didn't know your name was MacDougall when I saw you in the passage this morning. Or that this was so urgent."

"You should have left it where it was supposed to be left," he rebuked in a surly tone.

"I wasn't told that . . . only to give it to you. I'm sorry, but I've done as I was asked," Laura retaliated, lifting her chin.

He glowered at her. "Thanks," he muttered ungraciously, and turned his back rudely. He immediately buried his head in the truck's engine once more while the dog sprawled in the shade and eyed Laura suspiciously.

Laura stood her ground for a moment, biting her lip, torn half between fear of the dog and uncertainty of the man. Then she straightened her shoulders resolutely. She had taken a strong dislike to this rude, arrogant man, MacDougall, but nevertheless she had to ask him about her brother.

Chapter Two

Keeping a wary eye on the dog, who lay head on forepaws, watching her, Laura moved a few paces nearer to the truck.

She said hesitantly, "Excuse me, Mr. MacDougall . . ."

The blond head jerked up again and he glared at her in annoyance. "Can't you see I'm busy?" he snapped.

His tone riled her. "Yes," she retorted smartly. "I don't imagine you bury your head in truck engines for light entertainment!"

His eyes narrowed dangerously. Hands on hips, he regarded her derisively. "Right," he drawled, "I don't. Well, what is it? I told you Fogarty . . ."

His eyes challenged her and she felt about as small as an ant.

"I understand that you take supplies to Professor Fairchild," Laura said, coming straight to the point.

His expression remained as though carved from granite. "What if I do?" He peered at her suspiciously.

"I should like to go with you on this trip," she stated calmly.

For a moment he looked completely taken aback. Then he laughed loudly. "I'm not running a tourist service."

"I know. I just want to see Professor Fairchild."

He considered her for a moment, then his mouth twisted contemptuously. "So you're one of those slick city reporters who thinks she's on to a story, are you? Well, you can forget it. He's not talking. To anyone."

His harsh tone was utterly uncompromising. She guessed that Eric must have been bothered previously by journalists anxious to know what he was doing and why, hoping for a story. She knew he would shun all kinds of publicity. His work was strictly scientific, not sensational popular paper stuff.

Nevertheless, she could not help a sudden devilish urge to bait this overconfident man a little. "He'll talk to *me*," she informed him airily.

He smiled, but it wasn't friendly. His eyes crawled over her, taking in every detail of her slight frame. "That's what they always say," he replied acidly. "But being glamorous and sexy won't persuade the Prof to talk, so I'd go straight back to whichever gossipy little rag you've come from and tell 'em, no go."

Laura did not move. She faced him boldly. "You are too hasty in your conclusions, Mr. MacDougall. I am not a journalist. I'm Professor Fairchild's sister."

She watched with some relish as he digested this, to him, startling statement. Clearly it was the last thing he had expected her to say. He looked, however, as though he didn't believe her, and grinned maliciously.

"Neat ruse . . . but it won't work. I'm not that easily taken in." He laughed derisively. "You, the Prof's sister! I'd take bets she's the last person to come looking for him here. If you're Professor Fairchild's sister, I'm a Dutchman!"

Laura, seething, flipped open her bag, fumbled for her passport, opened it and thrust it under his nose. "You're a Dutchman!" she said, drawing her lips together and regarding him with a self-satisfied smirk.

He glanced at the details and the photograph. "Laura

21

Fairchild . . ." He read her name, then looked at her.
'You're not in the least like him." He still seemed unwilling
to believe she was telling the truth.

"No," she agreed, keeping her temper with difficulty. "We
aren't alike at all. We had the same father but different
mothers." To be fair, she could understand his doubt. Eric
was a large well-built man with the bushy red hair and beard
of their father, while she had inherited none of the physical
characteristics of her father, only his deep greenish-brown
eyes and his quicksilver temper. Physically she was a younger
less sophisticated edition of her glamorous mother.

MacDougall regarded her suspiciously. "What brings you
out here? The Prof doesn't have much time for his family, I
gather."

Laura flinched. "He . . . he didn't care much for my
mother, I'm afraid. He . . . he had good reason." She
paused, and bit her lip. Suddenly it was hard to say it. "My
mother died a short while ago. Eric is . . . practically my only
relative. . . ." It sounded so improbable, so lame. She waited
for him to ask her about her mother's family and dreaded
trying to explain. Her lip trembled. The full impact of total
loneliness could wash over her so unexpectedly, as it was
doing now. This man was enough to make anyone feel alone
and unwanted.

A muscle twitched at the corner of his mouth, but there was
no discernible sympathy in his tone as he said, "I'll take him a
message if you like."

She found her gaze trapped by the steely gray eyes. She
shook her head. "No, I want to see him myself. . . . I'd like
to come with you. . . ."

"Not bloody likely," he returned at once.

Laura recoiled. "Why not?" she demanded. "He's my
brother. I've got a right to see him. . . ." She trailed away,
quelled by the intensity of his gaze.

He folded his arms across his broad chest. "Your rights
don't come into it," he told her bluntly. "I decide who goes
with me in the truck, and if you think I'm going to take the
Prof's plummy-voiced little pommy sister to pay a social call
on him, you're out of your mind. What do you expect to do

when you get there, sit down and sip tea out of a bone-china cup? Besides, I'll be on the road for a week or more. You'd never stick it."

Laura felt rather dashed but she persisted. "It's very important to me to see Eric. . . ." There was no way she could explain her deeper feelings, her desperate need to talk to him, at this moment, and even if she could, she doubted this man would understand. He was not the sensitive type.

He took a pipe out of his overalls pocket and began to fill it with tobacco from a packet. "Now, look here, Miss Fairchild, be reasonable. If you want to send your brother a message, I'll take it. I take the mail anyway. Maybe he'll decide to come back with me to see you." He looked doubtful of this likelihood.

Laura could see that it was pointless to argue. He was implacable and there was no way she could make him change his mind. Tears welled up in her eyes in spite of herself. She ought to have known this might happen.

"Crying won't get you anywhere," MacDougall said callously. "Just look at it my way, will you? If the Prof's cut himself off from his family he won't thank me for dumping you on him. I don't want to get involved, thank you very much."

"I just want to talk to him," Laura said, desperately, "and there's no other way of getting to him. . . ."

MacDougall eyed her speculatively. "Do you know how he lives, Miss Fairchild? He lives with the aborigines, as near to like them as makes no difference. I take him medical supplies and flour once a month. He hasn't got a fancy house and servants to take in his poor little orphan half-sister, or perhaps you hadn't realized that. This is Outback Australia, you know."

She was angry at his inferences. "I know! I'm not a complete idiot, Mr. MacDougall, no matter what you think. I didn't come here to sponge on Eric. I am quite capable of looking after myself. I . . . I just want to see him."

His smile showed he knew he had touched a raw nerve. Had he? Laura winced. What did she expect of Eric that she had not been brave enough to admit even to herself? Did she expect him to do something concrete for her? She realized now that, although the thought had not crystallized, the expectation had been there all the time. She had always had other people to direct her life. It made her angrier than ever that this horrible man had winkled it out.

He spoke. "No, I will not take you. Write to him and leave your letter at the post office. I'll be collecting the mailbag this afternoon, straight after lunch. I'll bring you an answer in a week or so, if you care to stick around that long." He glanced around him, and added, "There isn't much to do in Camel Creek for a la-di-da young lady, I'm afraid." He puffed leisurely on his pipe.

Laura tried one last desperate plea. "I'll pay you well . . . whatever you ask . . . if you'll take me. How much . . . ?"

She instantly saw her mistake. His lip curled with contempt.

"No!" said the voice flatly. "I said no and I mean no. It's not on, and if you had a grain of sense in your head, you'd see why. I wouldn't accept the responsibility for one thing . . ." He paused, and added, emphatically, ". . . and for another, you can't buy MacDougall."

"I wouldn't hold you responsible for anything," Laura said, ignoring his second rebuff.

He sneered. "No? Well, I don't take that kind of risk, Miss Fairchild."

"What risk?" she persisted, determined to wear him down. "What could possibly happen?"

He shrugged. "Anything. You might break a leg, fall ill, get bitten by a snake, a dozen things. . . ." He glared at her. "It's no use your trying to twist my arm. I am not taking you and that is final. Now, if you don't mind, I'll get on with my job. I've got to get this truck ready to leave this afternoon. Good day." He knocked out his pipe on the side of the truck, returned it to his pocket and buried his head in the engine again.

Laura drew her lips together in a tight line. She stood there for a moment, seething with anger and disappointment. Then she turned and walked slowly back to the hotel, defeated.

Mrs. Burdekin was at the reception desk. "Well, dear, you

were a long time. Did you find MacDougall?" she asked pleasantly.

Laura nodded.

"Did he have any news of your brother?"

"Yes, but he refused to take me to see him."

Mrs. Burdekin seemed surprised that Laura had even contemplated going. "You wouldn't enjoy the run, dear. It's very rugged country, and I don't suppose MacDougall thinks you'd care for it." She pursed her lips slightly. "Not quite the thing for a young girl like you, anyway. I know I'm old fashioned and you young things do practically anything these days, but you'd be on the road a week or more with him. . . ." She trailed off, but her meaning was plain.

Laura had never given the slightest thought to the possible impropriety of her request, and was a little startled.

"He might be going to Nilla Nilla for a few days this time," went on Mrs. Burdekin, "before he comes back here." She explained, "That's his station. I expect he thought it would be too inconvenient for you."

Laura was curious despite herself. "Mr. MacDougall owns a cattle station?"

Mrs. Burdekin seemed half to regret having divulged this. "Yes. He doesn't spend much time there now, though. Just checks with his manager from time to time. He's in the trucking business now—not in any big way, just the mail run and a few contracting jobs locally." She shrugged. "Odd life really for a man like him, but . . ."

"He's an odd man," put in Laura with a wry smile.

The hotel proprietress became faintly defensive. "He's a good bloke, Miss Fairchild. One of the best." She gave Laura a narrow look. "But he doesn't have a lot of time for women these days. No young lady's going to pin MacDougall down. More's the pity, I say. Young Mac could do with a bit of softening around the edges. There's a bitter streak to him . . . but I suppose it's hardly any wonder—"

She did not finish, because someone came in and called to her. She broke off and said to Laura, "Go and have your breakfast, dear. Mavis is still about."

Laura, feeling rather hungry now, went into the now

deserted dining room. Mavis served her cheerfully, but thankfully without curiosity. No doubt she expected to learn all she wanted to know about the English visitor from her employer.

After breakfast Laura went up to her room and reluctantly started to write to Eric. She found it even more difficult to tell him she was in Camel Creek than it had been to write from England in the first place. The reckless impetuosity with which she had acted had been brought home to her fully this morning. A few cutting words from MacDougall had reduced her to size, she thought ruefully. Now she began to feel guilty for coming at all.

Back in London it had seemed brave and romantic and she had boosted her morale with visions of Eric's amazed joy when he saw her. Now she was not so sure. Perhaps he would, as MacDougall had hinted, be dismayed to see her, even angry. Suddenly she remembered the rows at home when she was younger and how he had stormed out vowing never to come back. He had cut himself off from them, and yet Laura could not believe he would not be pleased to see her. There were, after all, all those birthday cards. . . .

Laura chewed her pen thoughtfully and screwed up several sheets of writing paper. She just didn't know how to explain her desperate need to see him and talk to him. It was hot in the room so she turned on the fan. Its huge blades knifed the warm air and sent a cooler draft down onto her. Laura screwed up yet another sheet of paper. She had no right, she suddenly thought, to expect Eric to leave his work and travel into Camel Creek to see her. For what? Just so that she could unburden her soul to him, ask his advice, cry on his shoulder. That was being immature and selfish. Perhaps it would be better if she simply left and wrote from home as she should have done in the first place. It was unfair to burden Eric with her problems. She must find her own solutions. She stared at the hard blue sky through the window and the emptiness yawned terrifyingly before her. She bent her head on her arms and wept silently for a few minutes.

Eventually, she pulled herself together. She would not write to Eric. She would make one last attempt to persuade

MacDougall to take her with him. If she failed, then she would return south on the next bus. With renewed resolution she went out to find the big blond man who stood between her and what she wanted most in the world at that moment. She would convince him that it was more sensible to take her to see Eric than to expect him to come in to Camel Creek.

She strolled across to the garage, hoping to find that he was still tinkering with the truck, but he was nowhere around, nor was the truck. A man approached her.

"Looking for someone, miss? Jack Fogarty's the name."

"I was looking for Mr. MacDougall," Laura said.

He gave her a sly smile. "MacDougall, eh? And what would you be wanting with him?"

"I . . . I just want a quick word with him," she answered. "He was here this morning. Do you know where he is now?"

He looked her over and there was a twinkle in his eyes as he said, "He'll be at the store most likely, loading up supplies. He'll not be in the mood for flirtation, though. He's a week late and there's fellows out bush running low on rations. He'll be anxious to get away."

"I won't delay him," said Laura, with dignity.

Jack Fogarty grinned. "If I was him I'd be sorry about that!" He pointed down the street. "You'll find the store that way."

Laura muttered hurriedly, "Thanks," and sped off, conscious of his inquisitive gaze following her.

MacDougall's truck was parked outside the general store. At least, she mused, walking toward it, you didn't have to look far for anyone in this town. You could walk right around the whole settlement in five minutes.

MacDougall was nowhere to be seen, but a man was loading boxes and bags into the back of the truck. The dog, Caesar, was supervising, judging by his faithful following of every movement. When Laura approached, the man paused and grinned at her in a friendly fashion.

"Hello," she said. "Is Mr. MacDougall about?" Her courage was already beginning to falter as she remembered how implacable he had been this morning. Was he likely to be any less so now?

The man jerked his head toward the front of the store. "He's inside, collecting the mail."

Laura realized that the store was also the post office.

"Thanks," she said, and walked into the dim cool interior of the general store. Coming in from the glare outside she could not at first see a thing, and then she was aware of being observed by two people—one of whom was MacDougall. The other, a stout woman with dyed blond hair, was behind the counter. A lean black dog came out from behind it and barked at Laura.

"Dusky . . . that'll do!" rebuked the woman, and the dog subsided, eyeing Laura warily.

MacDougall shot her a look of total indifference. He turned back to the woman. "Well, if that's the lot, Mrs. Lawson, I'll be off. Just got to get my gear from the pub and have a bite of lunch. See you soon!" He dipped his rather battered slouch hat.

"See you, Mac," said Mrs. Lawson. "Regards to all the folks." She smiled a greeting at Laura as he turned away. "Can I help you?"

Laura quickly stood in the man's way. "Mr. MacDougall . . ." she said firmly.

He crushed her with a glance. "Now what? Haven't you posted your letter? I told you I'd be collecting the mail this afternoon." He pushed past her, walking through the door. "Well, you'd better let me have it," he said irritably.

She followed. "I haven't written yet," she said. "I . . ."

He glanced at her, eyebrows raised. "Changed your mind, have you?"

"I don't want to bring Eric all the way here to see me," said Laura. "I don't think it's fair to drag him away from his work."

A half-smile flickered across his lips. "I bet it's not often you consider someone other than yourself."

Laura resisted the urge to slap him. What a boor he was!

"I still want to come with you," she said stubbornly.

He heaved the bags he was carrying into the truck, then faced her. "I'm afraid you must excuse me, Miss Fairchild. I'm in rather a hurry." His icy politeness chilled her. He opened the cabin door and was about to get in when she tugged desperately at his sleeve. "Please . . . please take me with you. I promise I'll be no trouble. I just want to see Eric. . . ." Tears filled her eyes as she added emotionally. "He's all I've got. . . ."

She was immediately ashamed of this display of sentiment and knew he thought her either foolish and weak, or putting on a scene for his benefit. This made her angrier than ever with him, but just for a moment, as their eyes met, she was sure there was a glimmer of reluctant sympathy in those stony gray depths. However, it was gone almost as it appeared.

"No," he replied coldly. "Now, will you please leave me alone. I haven't got time to argue with you. I'm not taking you and that's all there is to it. If you want to send a message I'll be here until I've had my lunch."

Caesar jumped up into the truck's cabin and MacDougall sprang up after him and slammed the door. Laura stood beside it and clenched her fists. The truck moved slowly along the street and turned up into the side street alongside the hotel.

Defeated again, she followed. She saw MacDougall park the truck in the shade of an old she-oak at the side of the hotel and then hurry back and through the front entrance. Laura walked disconsolately into the hotel after him. Caesar had sprawled on the doormat, and lifted one eye to glance at her as she stepped over him. Laura supposed that Mac-Dougall would have gone straight into the dining room. Glancing through the door, she saw she was right. He was on the far side of the room and Mavis was already taking his order. She could not bear to be in the same room with him so she went on upstairs, intending to have her lunch later when he had gone.

From her bedroom window she could see the truck down in the lot. As she looked down at it she was struck by a sudden daring idea. She caught her breath. The truck was well out of sight, far from prying eyes in the dining room and bar, or the main street. In fact it was highly unlikely that anyone would see her at this hour if . . .

Her heart began to race nervously, but there was no time

to weigh up the consequences or even consider the problems. If she was going to do it, she must act now. Spurred by her deep-rooted desire to see Eric in spite of the arrogant, smug MacDougall, she decided she would go whether he liked it or not. She would teach him to be hardhearted and uncooperative. She would stow away in his truck.

Without waiting for doubts to assail her, she grabbed her handbag, then seeing her toilet bag on the washstand she shoved that into it, picked up her cardigan and white cotton sun hat, and fled down the backstairs which brought her out very near to the truck and hidden from the view of anyone except someone who might chance to come down the stairs behind her.

The back of the truck was covered by a tentlike green tarpaulin on a metal frame and the back flaps were not tied. Swiftly looking around, Laura threw her handbag and hat and cardigan into the back of the truck, then heaved herself up over the tailboard and dropped down inside, too. There was very little room between the load and the tailboard and Laura knew that she risked discovery if she stayed there anyway, so she rearranged a few boxes and made herself a hiding place behind them, hoping MacDougall would not notice.

Crouched uncomfortably in this small space, she seemed to wait interminably, and when voices eventually came to her from outside, her heart began to beat so fast and loud she was sure MacDougall would hear it.

"Yep, all set," said MacDougall, answering an inquirer. "I'll be off now."

Laura held her breath as one of the flaps was pulled aside and MacDougall stowed his personal gear in the back of the truck. He did not seem to notice that some items had been moved around.

Laura then heard him say, "What's up, Caesar? Down boy! No, you don't ride in the back, you ride up front like always." He laughed suddenly. "Come on, stop sniffing around there, your tucker's on board, don't worry!"

Laura went rigid as she heard the dog snuffling outside the truck. Caesar knew she was in there, she felt sure, and was trying to tell MacDougall. Any minute now she would be discovered and her last chance of reaching Eric gone. She could see MacDougall's shadow as he fastened the tarpaulin flaps securely and then, to her relief, he said, "Come on Caesar. Up, boy. We're off now."

A moment later, the engine began to throb and then Laura felt the truck backing slowly out of the hotel lot. She swallowed hard. She had gotten away with it. A smile of jubilation spread across her face as she sank back against a sack of flour and relaxed. .

Chapter Three

For some minutes after the truck had started off on its journey Laura sat feeling almost childishly pleased with herself for her audacity, and even more elated at her success in outwitting MacDougall.

The only drawback was imagining his fury when he discovered her, as eventually he must. Although, carried away by the daring of her exploit, she had not at first given that fact a thought, she knew that discovery was inevitable sooner or later. The crucial factor was that it must be later rather than sooner, when they were too far on their way for MacDougall to turn around and bring her back. His delayed departure, she thought, was a godsend, as he would be reluctant to lose any more time.

The truck bumped about a great deal but Laura managed to make herself reasonably comfortable by wedging herself in between the bags and boxes of supplies. It was fairly dim under the tarpaulin, but there were small plastic windows in it through which, despite a coating of red dust, she could see some of the passing scenery. It was hardly inspiring. The countryside was flat, featureless and practically treeless. The ground was stony and spattered with clumps of a wiry dull green grass, occasional bushes with bright yellow flowers and patches of straggling dusty green vines bearing small yellow fruits, which looked like melons of some kind.

Soon she began to feel very hot. Her clothes stuck to her and she had to wipe her face frequently with a handkerchief. Time passed very slowly, and, tired of staring through the small distorting panes of plastic, she eventually leaned back and closed her eyes.

"You are stark, raving mad, Laura Fairchild," she murmured to herself. "What on earth are you doing here in this truck with this ghastly man? You don't even know that Eric will be pleased to see you. He'll probably be as angry as MacDougall."

She grinned to herself suddenly. The thought had just entered her head that if only the girls at the elegant West End beauty salon could see her now! With her shirt and slacks damp with sweat, her expensive white sandals as covered in red dust as her bare feet with their carefully painted toenails, her makeup smudged and her glossy dark hair hanging damply about her face, she must look a real fright. She thought of them in their pale pink and blue uniforms, their own hair beautifully done, their hands and feet immaculate, attending to the face packs, manicures, massages and making up of a daily stream of customers. It seemed more than half a world away; it seemed incredible that she had ever spent her waking hours in such surroundings.

It was not long before Laura became exceedingly thirsty. The dust which seeped in through the gaps in the tarpaulin lashing made her throat drier and drier. It was after enduring this new discomfort for some time that she suddenly noticed the large white box with the lift-up lid at the rear of the truck. She immediately guessed it was a portable refrigerator. How civilized of MacDougall, she thought, as she wrenched it open eagerly.

Disappointment followed. There was only meat and cans of beer, as far as she could see. She did not like beer and in any case she had no opener for the cans, which were unfortunately not of the flip-top variety. She put the lid down and licked her lips. Then she caught sight of a cardboard box which said APPLES on the side. Although it might have contained anything but the fruit, she eagerly ripped open the top. The prospect of a big juicy apple was almost more than she could bear. She was also hungry, she now realized, having had no lunch.

To her delight layers of tissue paper suggested that the box was indeed full of apples. She reached in and closed her hand over a firm fruit. It was a bright green Granny Smith, and as she held it up, no apple had ever looked more beautiful, more appetizing. She sank her teeth into it and the juice dribbled down her chin. She felt as guilty as a kid caught stealing but it couldn't be helped. Even MacDougall wouldn't want her to die of thirst, she thought.

The apple refreshed her and helped to fill the void caused by hunger. The truck bumped on and on along the dusty dirt road. Laura peered out of the tiny windows again. There was more bush now, she noticed, and the country was slightly less flat, but she could not see very well because of the clouds of red dust that the truck was throwing up. Soon she was thirsty again so she ate another apple. Her body began to ache from the jolting about and she felt nauseous from time to time because of the bumping up and down and the dust that she swallowed.

Her earlier exultation evaporated and she began to wonder if the nightmare was ever going to end. Her watch told her that they had been traveling a couple of hours, but did MacDougall never want to stop? Half of her wished he would, just to ease her agony, but the other half said no, the farther they went without stopping, the less risk there was of her being discovered too soon.

She slumped back between the sacks and boxes and in spite of the discomfort, the heat and the insidious dust, she eventually fell asleep. She had not had much sleep last night, and two days on the bus, following the flight from England, had left her drained. Despite the jolting of the truck, she slept soundly.

Laura woke with a start, panic rising in her throat. She was in complete darkness. For a moment she had no recollection of where she was, but when realization dawned, she gave another start. The truck had stopped. She heard the cabin door slam and then MacDougall's voice. He was talking to the dog. As he drew near to the back of the truck, Laura froze. She squeezed herself up tightly in her hiding place, fearful he would discover her. She felt dreadfully hot and sticky, she was dying of thirst again and her head ached.

She dared not raise her head to see what was happening but she heard sounds that suggested MacDougall was unlashing the tarpaulin flaps at the back. He was saying, "Okay, tucker time, Caesar. Just as soon as we get the fire going. But first I'm going to have a beer and I reckon you could do with a tin of water, eh?"

Laura tried to make herself even smaller as she heard MacDougall fumbling for the dog's tin. Then she heard water splashing into it, followed by Caesar's greedy slurping. There must be a water tank beneath the truck, she thought, and wondered how she could get a drink of water without being seen. She would have to use her hands for a cup, she thought, consumed with the desire for it.

Next she heard the lid of the fridge being lifted and a can being removed, the hiss as MacDougall opened it, the sigh of satisfaction as he downed the cold liquid. Her tongue burned worse than ever.

MacDougall said, "That's better, eh, Caesar?" Suddenly he laughed. "You know, old boy, we nearly copped a passenger this trip. Damn fool girl! Talk about wet behind the ears. She'd have been dead of the heat in five minutes, I'll bet. No, I reckon I was right not to risk bringing her. She'd have been a perishin' nuisance. Typical woman, full of lip but not a brain in her silly painted head."

Laura cringed. She held her breath wondering what other disparaging things he would say about her to the dog, but he moved away, presumably to light the fire. Soon he would be back for the food, but meanwhile Laura had discovered a need even more urgent than a drink or avoiding discovery. She would have to slip out of her hiding place somehow.

She crept up to the tailboard and apprehensively peered out. At first all she could see in the darkness were the faint

35

shapes of trees. The truck was parked in a clearing in the bush. She leaned out a little and glimpsed the flicker of firelight. The fire, she decided, was to one side near the front of the truck. MacDougall was, temporarily at least, unable to see the rear of the truck. Faintly she could hear him whistling, and she smiled rather wryly. She wondered if he knew he was whistling a very romantic ballad.

Her heart in her mouth, expecting him to appear at any moment, or Caesar to come bounding after her, Laura climbed down from the truck. She pressed herself flat against the side of the truck away from where MacDougall was and considered her next move. It was a few yards to the shelter of the scrub, but eventually she plucked up courage to run out into the open toward it. She would stay hidden there, she decided, until MacDougall was eating his supper, and then scramble back to her hiding place in the truck. If she could remain undetected until tomorrow, then surely it would be too late for MacDougall to take her back to Camel Creek. He would have to let her go along with him whether he liked it or not.

She shuddered apprehensively as she plunged into the thick scrub, but her fear of discovery overcame her fear of what might be lurking there. Her feet seemed to crackle loudly on dry twigs and she was sure MacDougall would come to investigate, but his placid whistling still drifted to her from over on the other side of the truck. Peering through the gloom she saw him return to the rear of the truck, presumably to take something out of the fridge. She ducked down and waited until he had gone back to the fire.

A few moments later, emerging from behind a large bush, zipping up her slacks, she started nervously at a slight sound, and then froze as she found herself face to face with Caesar, who began to snarl in a very unfriendly way.

Laura let out an involuntary scream and then realized that striding up behind Caesar was MacDougall. She could not see his eyes, only the dark sockets, but she knew they raked her searingly and that he was furious. She could only stand there frozen to the spot.

"Back, Caesar," murmured MacDougall. "Back . . . back . . ."

The dog instantly obeyed. MacDougall moved closer to the trembling Laura. "What the hell do you think you're playing at?" he demanded, grabbing her roughly by the arm. His eyes burned into hers at uncomfortably close quarters.

Laura drew a deep breath and determined not to be intimidated by him. "I want to see my brother," she said stubbornly.

He almost threw her from him. "I want. . . ." he echoed scathingly. "Your theme song, no doubt. You've been too used to getting your own way, obviously. Like your mother. Frivolous and selfish, so the Prof told me once, spending your father's money as though it was going out of fashion."

Laura's anger mounted. "I'm not like that!"

He ignored this protest. He faced her quivering form with arms folded, a laconic smile on his lips. "So you stowed away in the truck to get your own way this time. Did you imagine you could remain hidden until we got there?" he asked sarcastically.

She held his gaze, although it made her tremble. "No," she admitted honestly. "I . . . I just hoped to hide until it was too late for you to take me back." She wondered where she found the temerity to stand up to this man. She was determined, however, that he would not know how violently she was quaking inside.

His gaze was formidable. He said, "I ought to put you over my knee and tan the pants off you!"

She jumped back. "Don't you dare!"

Suddenly he laughed. "Well, you've got nerve, I'll say that for you, Miss Fairchild."

"My name is Laura." She attempted a friendly smile, hoping he was thawing a little.

He ignored her overture. He said brusquely, "Well, you'd better have some supper." The faintest of smiles glimmered on his lips as he added, "And next time you need to obey a call of nature, check with me first. I don't want you treading on a snake, or falling down an old mine shaft, or getting lost!"

It was perhaps premature, she knew, but Laura felt a rush of triumph as she followed him to the campfire. She crossed her fingers and hoped that he would accept her now. Caesar loped beside them, casting glances in her direction as though he was not sure what his master expected of him where she was concerned.

There was a frying pan on the coals. Sausages and hunks of bread were smoking in it. The delicious smell made Laura's parched mouth water involuntarily, and the hollowness inside her became a real hunger pain.

MacDougall stopped and turned to face her, his expression grim. "I don't suppose you had the forethought to tell Mrs. Burdekin where you were going?"

Laura looked sheepish. "No . . . of course not . . . I just came. . . ."

"I thought so. Well, as you obviously haven't the wit to realize, the whole of Camel Creek is probably combing the countryside for you. Your disappearance would scarcely go unnoticed, and the only thing that could have happened, they are sure to think, is that the foolish little English girl wandered off and got lost. They'll be none too pleased at having their time wasted."

Laura was appalled. Such a possibility had never occurred to her. "I . . . I didn't think of that. . . ." She faltered. "I'm sorry."

He spoke impatiently. "No, you wouldn't think, would you? You've lived all your cushy life in a nice cozy little cocoon, letting other people think for you. Spoiled rotten!"

"That's not fair!" she retorted. "I've done nothing of the sort. You've got quite the wrong idea. I earn my own living! You've no right to judge me by what you've heard about my mother."

He looked skeptical, but said, "And what do you do for a living?"

"I am a beautician."

The words were scarcely uttered before the grin spread over his face and he erupted into contemptuous laughter. "Beautician! I might have guessed it would be something useless and frivolous like that! Yes," he added, peering at her, "it suits you." Then he strode toward the truck, saying, "Luckily I carry a radio. I can let Camel Creek know that the irresponsible Miss Fairchild is safe." He called over his shoulder, "See to the tucker. You'd better throw on another link of sausages and slice some more bread." He added sarcastically, "I don't suppose it occurred to you to bring your own rations."

Like Caesar, Laura obeyed without question. MacDougall, she reflected, was a man who commanded obedience. She seethed inwardly at his contempt for her profession. He might laugh at it, but it was darned hard work sometimes, both physically and mentally. Often she was on her feet all day, and being pleasant to the often not very pleasant customers was frequently a strain.

However, feeling rather chastened, she rummaged in the pack near the fire and cut off two sausages from a string. She had better not eat too much, she thought, and risk being labeled greedy as well as irresponsible. She felt very guilty now because she had not given a thought to the concern her disappearance might cause. Well, it was his fault, she justified stubbornly. If he had agreed to her coming in the first place, she would have told Mrs. Burdekin, and what's more she would have brought her own provisions.

She turned out the already cooked sausages onto the tin plate she saw standing ready, and placed it at the edge of the fire to keep hot while she cooked the others, shaking them about in the pan and turning the hunks of bread so that they wouldn't burn. Caesar watched from a distance, tongue lolling.

In a few minutes, MacDougall returned. He towered over Laura. "I called them up. They were only just beginning to panic. You weren't missed until dinner time, it seems, and there's not much they could do in the dark anyway."

Laura glanced up at him contritely. "I'm sorry, I . . ."

He squatted on the other side of the fire. "So you damn well ought to be. I ought to run you straight back tonight."

She pursed her lips but did not dare say anything.

He went on, "I damn well ought to, but that would mean another day's delay."

She couldn't help the smile that flew to her lips. "You're going to let me stay then . . . ?"

"Only because I'm more of a bloody fool than I should be," he growled. "I just can't afford to waste the time. If you behave yourself and don't cause me any trouble, okay, but if you do, I might just decide to let you find your own way back." He glowered at her.

Laura bent her head and shivered. He couldn't mean that, of course. He was just trying to frighten her, but the feeling of exultation at having outwitted him was nevertheless diminished by the feeling of unease. He was a hard, uncompromising man and might find ways to punish her anyway. MacDougall, she felt sure, was capable of anything.

"You don't get treated with kid gloves, either," he told her firmly, "just because you happen to be a woman. You chose to come so you can put up with it. I don't want to hear any complaints because this isn't luxury tourist travel."

Laura stifled a hot retort. She said mildly, "Do you want your food now?"

She met his gaze steadily. It was still stony and disapproving. "Yep," he answered shortly.

"I kept your plate hot," Laura said, grabbing the edge with her handkerchief, to pass it to him.

He said gruffly, "You can have the plate. I'll eat out of the frying pan."

She tilted her head and gave him as arch a smile as she could summon. "I thought you said there was to be no chivalry."

His eyes darted swiftly to her face. She could see he was battling not to allow a smile to spoil his gruffness. "There isn't. I'll have the freshly cooked grub," he said. "The first lot is a bit dried up." He grabbed the frying pan handle, adding, "Only one set of cutlery. Which do you want, knife or fork?" He held them out to her.

Laura ignored the offer. "I'll eat with my fingers," she said airily, and picked up a sausage.

"I don't carry paper napkins," he mocked.

"Good, they're a waste of trees," she replied promptly, and caught a swift, rather surprised glance from him. She also

40

noticed that by taking the frying pan he now had less food than she did, so she held out the plate. "I think some of this is yours."

He made no move to take any of it. "I think your need is greater than mine," he said. "I had lunch and you didn't."

"I'm not—" she began.

"Eat it," he commanded, and then added peremptorily, "See to the tea."

Laura moved the primitive tin kettle onto the center of the coals. In spite of MacDougall she was rather enjoying herself now. The crisis was over and she felt almost relaxed. Mac-Dougall might be surprised, she thought, to discover that she had done quite a lot of camping out in her teens, and roughly too. That had been when she had fallen in with a group who were crazy about getting back to nature. It hadn't lasted long though. Her mother, who had always dominated her, had been horrified and had put a stop to it. Laura sighed. Why had she allowed herself to be pushed around so much? Well, it didn't matter now. She looked up at the stars and was suddenly reminded of how good it had felt before, out in the open, sleeping under the sky. She was glad she had come. And she would show this arrogant Australian she was no sissy English miss, but as tough as he was.

The sausages she was eating were slightly black on one side where they had been left while he went to see what Caesar was after, but they tasted good. Absently wiping her greasy fingers on the end of her boutique shirt, Laura caught MacDougall's eye, and the tail end of a laconic smile.

He put down the frying pan and wiped his hand across his mouth. "Not bad," he allowed grudgingly. "You can cook a decent sausage, so you'll be some use, I suppose."

Laura was not expecting even a backhanded compliment. "Thanks," she said, and then, "shall I pour your tea?"

He regarded her with amusement, and she knew he was gloating over her eagerness to please, and placate. He would take full advantage of her obligation to him throughout the trip, she thought a little ruefully. But it would be worth it if she got to see Eric, she consoled herself.

"I've got another mug somewhere," MacDougall said, and

strode over to the truck, returning a minute later with a second enamel mug, rather chipped and stained and very dusty. He handed it to her. "Best I can do."

Laura hid her instinctive revulsion for the grubby stained mug. She rinsed the dust out of it with a drop of tea and then filled both mugs, splashing some into the fire in her clumsy way.

She handed MacDougall his. She felt the rough skin of his fingers touch hers briefly as the mug exchanged hands and a shiver ran down her spine. Their eyes locked for a moment, and she looked quickly away. For the first time the full impact of her situation dawned. She was all alone in the middle of nowhere with a man she did not know. She was completely in his power, and his look said quite plainly that he was well aware of it.

Laura sipped her scalding tea. There was a silence between them for some minutes. "How long have you been doing this run?" she asked when the atmosphere became too charged for her comfort.

The firelight played on his face, the flickering shadows making it look now malevolent, now curiously kind. He took his time about answering, then said briefly, "Couple of years."

"What did you do before?" She hoped he might tell her about his cattle station, but he did not.

"None of your business." His tone resented her curiosity.

"Sorry . . ." She wasn't and thought he was rude, so she recklessly needled him. "I guess if you'd been in jail, you wouldn't want to talk about it."

He regarded her without humor, and his mouth tightened. "Clever, aren't you? I have never been in jail so if you're trying to sniff out a sensational story for your paper, you won't get one from me."

Laura was astonished. "I'm not a reporter," she said. "I told you, I'm Eric's sister. You saw my passport."

"That mightn't stop you being a journalist," he answered doggedly, and she felt like laughing. He added, "You don't act much like the kind of sister I imagined him to have."

"Oh?" she said. "I thought that was exactly what I was doing according to your earlier remarks."

"I don't see the kind of girl his sister'd be stowing away in a truck, or tossing sausages in a pan."

Laura had to laugh. "My goodness, you do have some strange ideas about Eric's sister. I can't imagine what he must have told you."

"He didn't tell me anything—about you."

"Well, you must have some funny ideas about women, then," Laura said.

"I daresay," he acknowledged in a dry tone.

There was a silence once more. MacDougall took out his pipe, slowly filled it and lit it. He glanced across at Laura. "Smoke?"

"No."

"Sensible. Pipe's all right, though. Keeps the flies off and the mossies." He added, as she slapped at a mosquito on her arm, "Stick close to the fire and they won't bother you."

Laura had begun to feel cold in spite of the fire. She rose. "I think I'll get my cardigan."

When she came back he had banked the fire up and it was crackling nicely, throwing out a good warmth.

Laura took up her former position. "I never realized it would be cold at night. I thought it would be hot all the time in Central Australia."

He puffed slowly, the pipe smoke mingling with the acrid smoke from the fire. "It can drop to freezing and below some nights in winter."

Laura had been considering a problem. "Where do you sleep?" she asked tentatively.

His look was inscrutable. "In the back of the truck, when there's room."

Laura digested this without comment, wondering where he would expect her to sleep.

He gave a low chuckle. "I guess you'd object to sharing my blanket! Well, lucky for you I've got a spare sleeping bag. A mate of mine left a better one behind, so you can have my old one and sleep in the truck. I'll sleep on the ground."

Laura answered haughtily, "There's no need to be chivalrous. I thought you said you wouldn't be. I can sleep on the ground."

"Suit yourself," he said, and then added, "I'll be turning in shortly. I want to kick off again at dawn."

"How long before we reach Eric?" Laura asked.

"Depends where they are. If they've moved on, as is likely since the last time, he'll have left a message for me. Could be two or three days."

"Who will they leave a message with?" Laura asked.

"Nobody. I know where to find it."

"Where do you stop first?" Laura asked.

MacDougall did not seem to resent her questions, rather to her surprise.

"We drop off mail at a couple of stations tomorrow," he told her, "deliver supplies to a mining camp and an old prospector, and a couple more outlying stations." He grinned at her. "We'll be quite busy."

Again they fell silent. The fire burned low and finally MacDougall tapped out his pipe on the end of a branch that had not been completely burned in the fire. He stood up, "Better turn in—if you're going to be any use tomorrow."

Laura scrambled up, hugging her cardigan around her against the sharp cold that made her shiver as she moved away from the warmth of the fire. Her eyes met his, and caught a fleeting expression that belied the disparagement in his voice. Or perhaps it was just a trick of the firelight, she thought, turning hastily away, disturbed by the extraordinary feeling that to have the arms of a man like MacDougall around you would be the most wonderfully safe feeling in the world.

She waited for him to move, but he just stood there on the other side of the fire between her and the truck, his feet half a stride apart, his arms folded across his broad chest, his chin arrogantly tilted as he regarded her. He was deliberately trying to disconcert her, she felt certain. His lips shaped a smiling taunt, his whole stance declared his control of the situation, of her, and yet, although she wanted to run wildly away from the consequences of her rashness, his undeniable male magnetism sent a curiously pleasurable tremor through her.

At last, without speaking again, he turned and strolled over to the truck. Laura followed and stood uncertainly nearby as he rummaged around for a moment or two under the tarpaulin. Eventually he emerged and tossed a sleeping bag and a gray blanket onto the floor at the back of the truck where there was a clear space.

In the darkness she could not see the expression in his eyes, but when he spoke there was an odd breathiness in his voice, and it almost trembled, even as he rapped out peremptorily, "Okay, now get to bed!"

Laura jerked forward clumsily in her nervousness, and as he jumped down from the tailboard, his arm brushed against her cheek. She felt the softness of hair and the warmth of his skin against the coolness of her own, and she drew back as though burned.

"Sorry," he muttered curtly.

"Where . . . where are you going to sleep?" she asked hesitantly.

He was silent for a moment, then said rather scathingly, "I won't be far away—in case you're frightened of the dark!"

Laura glanced at the cramped floor space in the truck. She guessed he usually slept there himself. She felt conscience-stricken, pushing him out to sleep on the ground. No chivalry, he'd said.

She heard herself blurting out, "There'd be room for both of us if we just shifted a few of the boxes and sacks. . . ."

She should have known such a suggestion would be misconstrued. She regretted her impulse the minute the words were uttered. His face was shadowed, but she could feel the scorn emanating from him in the deathly silence that greeted her remark. She heard him draw in a deep breath, and then, without warning, he thrust himself at her, grasping her arms and pinioning her against the tailboard of the truck, his fingers digging into her upper arms, and his hard muscular body thwarting any resistance on her part.

"So that *is* your game," he rasped angrily, "that's really why you came along? You were looking for someone to molest you?"

"No . . . !" She was shocked, and not a little frightened of him, as his words whiplashed her, and his eyes, close to her face, blazed. She could feel his heartbeat against her, but it was steady and rhythmic, not racing wildly like her own. She had provoked him into a violent reaction but he was still in control.

"You're all the same, aren't you," he sneered. "You think no man can resist you!" There was a bitterness mingled with his wrath. His grip on her tightened as he said, ominously, "Well . . . perhaps you're right . . . !"

"You're hurting me. . . ." Laura squeezed out through clenched teeth.

He laughed, a short harsh sound without mirth. "Play with fire and you run the risk of getting burned . . . or hurt. . . ."

She had the strange feeling for a moment that he was using her to vent some long walled-up grudge that had really nothing to do with her at all. She struggled instinctively, but he held her imprisoned like a helpless bird and pressed closer against her while she went rigid with apprehension, knowing she had brought it on herself. She closed her eyes, feeling the sting of angry tears burning behind the lids.

And then, unexpectedly, his grip relaxed. Laura opened her eyes. His face was still uncomfortably close to hers, but there was now a faintly teasing smile on his lips although his shadowed eyes were still unfathomable.

He murmured in a soft husky voice, "Well . . . I suppose you do deserve some reward for your efforts. . . ."

Before she could even avert her face his mouth had claimed hers in a kiss that was momentarily brutal, then exquisitely sensuous. Laura's senses reeled; for a moment their sparring, his anger, her fear, were all forgotten, as her lips responded to his involuntarily, giving as he demanded, taking what he gave with a surge of feeling that engulfed her whole being and made her dizzy with an explosive kind of joy.

It was all too brief, a moment out of time, a taste of ecstasy that ended before she could believe it had happened. Surely that was not MacDougall's large brown hand that so lightly caressed the warm bare skin across the small of her back, MacDougall's mouth that lifted from hers reluctantly, his lips that now drifted tantalizingly across her own as though he would prolong the pleasure of their intimacy.

Dumbfounded, Laura remained limply in his arms, unable to resist, not even wanting to now. He seemed almost to be caught in the same kind of surprised state of suspended animation. But it did not last. Abruptly his tight hold on her was renewed, then he roughly pushed her to one side, releasing her, and saying in a voice that still bore traces of the passion he must now be angry with himself for revealing, "Get to bed before you tempt me to forget myself completely! And don't think what just happened meant anything, or is likely to happen again!"

His words were like ice-cold water dashed in her face. As he strode around to the side of the truck, Laura slumped against the tailboard, trembling.

"Oh!" she cried silently, slamming one tightly clenched fist into her other palm, "oh, how I hate him!"

She was about to climb up into the truck when, on an impulse, she changed her mind. She would at least show him she was not soft. No chivalry, he had said. Well, she wouldn't accept any, even when it was offered. She would sleep on the ground too. On the other side of the truck from him!

She rolled up the blanket to make a pillow, and then slid into the sleeping bag. It smelled faintly of him, his body and his pipe tobacco, but she did not mind. She felt strangely comforted by it and soon fell asleep.

Laura woke with a start. Something cold and damp was pressing against her cheek. She sat bolt upright at once, realized that it was daylight and that it was only Caesar waking her with a friendly lick. He flopped back on his haunches, tongue lolling, well satisfied with his success in rousing her. Then, as she blinked sleepily, her eyes focused on a pair of dusty boots, khaki trousers and, as she lifted her gaze, MacDougall standing over her with a mug of hot tea in his hand.

Chapter Four

Laura said, "Good morning!"

MacDougall put the mug of tea into her hand. "'Morning," he said gruffly.

"I . . . I'm sorry I slept so soundly," she apologized, clasping her hands around the hot mug and avoiding his eyes. The tea was strong and sweet and tasted much better than any she had ever drunk.

"I'm surprised you managed to," he commented, his steely gray gaze steady, giving nothing away. "I'd have thought you'd have been terrified of what might come crawling into your sleeping bag with you, on the ground." He paused, and there was a hint of ironic amusement in his next remark. "I meant snakes or spiders, of course."

Laura shuddered. She had been too shattered by what had happened last night, and too determined to prove to him that she did not have to be pampered, to even think of creepy-crawlies when she made her decision to sleep on the ground. He knew this, and laughed at the involuntary revulsion her face showed as she thought of it now.

"Ignorance can be bliss!" he observed, with a touch of malice.

Laura, thoroughly disconcerted by his formidable presence, looked around her. In the pale morning light everything seemed unreal—the pink washed sky, the skeletal trees, the shadowy undergrowth; even MacDougall, standing there, feet apart, like a monument to some dauntless pioneer, she thought fancifully, hard as granite, and as feelingless.

Feelingless? That wasn't true. She recalled his iron grip, the fierce pressure of his body against hers, the glitter in his eyes as they had come together for that brief passionate encounter in the starlight. MacDougall had feelings all right, dangerous ones so far as she was concerned. A shiver ran through her as she dared a glance at him, still standing watching her as she drank her tea, as though the picture fascinated him—or, more likely, he was just in a hurry to pack the mug away.

"You're ready to go?" she inquired.

"Yep."

Laura hastily gulped down the rest of her tea. He held out his hand for the mug. She felt guilty for holding him up and made up her mind that tomorrow she would be the first up. She would show him she was no liability.

He ordered crisply, "Stow your sleeping bag in the back. I'll fix the fire and then we'll be off. We'll stop for breakfast later."

He strode away, and Laura unzipped the sleeping bag and clambered out of it. Every muscle and bone in her body ached from sleeping on the hard ground. She felt grubby and sticky, and her clothes were badly crumpled. She longed for a warm shower and clean clothes, but she did not dare ask if there was any water to spare for a wash. MacDougall would be bound to sneer. So she kept silent and made do with combing her hair and trying to smooth out the worst creases in her pants and shirt. The red dust with which they were already ingrained, she could do nothing about.

In her handbag, seeing lipstick and powder, she automatically lifted out her compact and opened it, but the minute she saw her face, closed it again. If she made up, MacDougall would probably pour scorn on her, so with a defiant clamping of her jaws she put the makeup away, even rejecting the perfume atomizer she knew was in the bottom of her bag somewhere.

"If I don't smell nice," she muttered, "he can jolly well put up with it. I'll have to put up with him!"

She walked around to the front of the truck, hoping that MacDougall would have softened sufficiently to allow her to ride up front. She did not look forward to spending the entire trip being bumped around in the back of the truck. Even sitting beside the contemptuous MacDougall couldn't be worse than that.

However, she saw with some disappointment that Caesar was already occupying the passenger seat, his tongue lolling out, eager to be off. It looked as though MacDougall meant to punish her. The dog eyed Laura disdainfully, growling in answer to her friendly but wary greeting.

MacDougall was shoveling earth over the remains of the fire. He finished the job and then strode back to the truck and stowed the shovel. Laura stood waiting, looking around her. There was little to see except the bush, which hemmed them in on all sides. She could not even see the dirt road they were traveling on. MacDougall came over to her.

"You'll have to sit in the middle," he said shortly. "Caesar likes to poke his head out of the window to catch the breeze." He opened the passenger door and motioned Caesar to get down. "Out, boy!" Caesar obeyed. "Up you get," Mac-Dougall said to Laura in the same tone, as though she were a dog too.

The sky was changing from pink to gold when they pulled out of the clearing and back onto the road which was little better than a path. Laura sat stiffly and uncomfortably between the man and his dog, and wished sometimes that she had stayed in the back of the truck.

Caesar, accustomed to occupying the whole of the passenger seat, did not take kindly toward having to share it. He pushed heavily against her as he tried to maintain his usual position, half crouched, with his nose on the windowsill. His not inconsiderable weight tended to push Laura nearer and nearer to MacDougall, and every jolt of the truck meant she was thrown either against the dog or his master. MacDougall seemed disinclined to talk and Laura's efforts to make conversation mostly received only monosyllabic replies so that in the end she gave up and concentrated on watching the scenery.

Presently, the bush thinned and they began to cross a stretch of flat country with hills on the distant horizon, but otherwise unrelieved except for clumps of spiky grass and gnarled pinelike trees which MacDougall in a rare moment of communication told her were desert oaks up to a hundred years old or more. The grass, he said, was spinifex.

For ages it seemed that the hills swayed in the haze but never came any nearer, until midmorning when quite suddenly they were heading into hilly country and quickly becoming surrounded by rugged outcrops of red rock, some strangely shaped, all rather forbidding. They had stopped once on the plain to leave mail and a parcel in a box on a fence post, but there had been no sign of the station homestead it was intended for. Laura found it hard to believe that anyone could possibly enjoy living in such isolation and in such barren, featureless country.

When they stopped again it was not for a delivery. "Breakfast," said MacDougall briefly, and with just a suggestion of a grin. "Or perhaps I should say elevenses! Hungry?"

Laura nodded. She still felt guilty about eating his food but consoled herself that he must have plenty or he would have suggested rationing it. She also suspected that keeping her waiting for breakfast was all part of his plan to make the trip as unpleasant for her as possible. She gritted her teeth and determined she would show no sign of not thoroughly enjoying herself.

She was helping to pile up sticks for a fire to boil the kettle to prove she could be useful, when she suddenly stepped back in horror and let out a scream. A large scorpion was waving its antennae inches from her bare toes.

MacDougall strode over. "What's up?"

She pointed, too scared to speak or move. He kicked the scorpion aside with the toe of his boot, and it immediately turned its attention to him, taking up a threatening stance.

"Aren't you going to kill it?" Laura said, shakily, surprised that he was just standing there. Caesar loped over to investigate.

MacDougall glanced at her. "Kill it? Why?"

"Scorpions are poisonous, aren't they? It nearly stung me—"

She stopped on his look of utter contempt. "And just because of that you want me to stamp on it? Is that how you see life, stamping on anything that gets in your way? I suppose I shouldn't be surprised." His eyes narrowed. "No, I am not going to kill it. It wouldn't have killed you. This is its rightful environment. We are the intruders. It isn't the scorpion's fault you're wearing highly unsuitable footwear. I suggest that you look where you're going, especially in those ridiculous sandals."

"But Caesar might . . ." began Laura, rather put out by his attitude.

"Caesar won't interfere with a scorpion," said Mac-Dougall. "He has more sense."

Laura felt as if the scorpion had actually stung her. She lowered her gaze and felt rather ashamed. Then, unexpectedly, her anger at MacDougall dissipated and she looked at him curiously, seeing a facet of the man she had not suspected. She knew that her involuntary reaction to the scorpion was unnecessary and he was right. There was nothing she could say. And there was nothing she could do about her flimsy sandals. They were all she had.

MacDougall made the tea and Laura cut bread and folded it over slices of cheese. MacDougall sat on a log but she remained standing. Eventually he said, "You can sit down, Laura. There's nothing to bite you over here." His half-smile mocked her.

She sat as far from him as she could, sipped her tea and munched her sandwich hungrily. He did not speak again. A bird presently began to sing lustily in a tree just behind them.

Laura looked up, thrilled by the full-throated melodious sound, wondering what bird was making it.

"Pied butcher-bird," said MacDougall. "Little black and white fellow, one of our best songsters. Can't see him, though. . . . I'll try and tempt him down." He broke off a piece of cheese and threw it onto the ground under the tree. Almost immediately, the song ceased and a moment later there was a flash of wings as the butcher-bird dived to the ground. Laura saw it clearly as it retrieved the cheese and then flew to a lower branch of the tree.

"He's a handsome fellow," she observed. "He has a saucy eye!"

MacDougall gave a low chuckle. "He's a cadger. You'll always find butcher-birds coming around a camp. They like bacon rind, too."

As they watched, the strikingly plumaged little bird was joined by another that MacDougall said was his mate, and then a brownish one which to Laura looked quite different but which MacDougall said was a young one.

Laura tossed a few pieces of cheese to them and was rewarded by having them come up quite close to her. She was enchanted. She was also glad because the birds seemed to have caused MacDougall to mellow a little.

However, once they were back in the truck he was as moodily silent as before. They stopped twice to deliver mail, and it was well after midday when they arrived at the mining camp. Laura had not really had any preconceived notion of what a mining camp might be like, but she was a little surprised to find that it was not much more than a couple of tents, a rough wooden hut and a few gaunt pieces of machinery. It was situated in a very barren part of the range.

As the truck swung around and halted in a flurry of dust, three men came out of the tents.

"Cripes, Mac, where've you been?" demanded the first, grasping MacDougall's hand and pumping it hard as he jumped down from the truck.

Caesar immediately whined to be let out, so at a word from his master, Laura unfastened the passenger door. The dog was out like a flash. Laura heard one of the men say, "Got a passenger this trip, Mac?" He came over and looked into the cabin. "Blow me down, a girl!" He turned and winked at MacDougall. "Good for you, mate!"

MacDougall sneaked a sidelong, rather teasing look at Laura and said, "I'm just giving her a lift, Bill." They all looked skeptical and Laura felt stupidly embarrassed.

"Well, come and have a bite," said Bill. "We've been taking bets for the last three days you'd arrive by lunchtime— we were beginning to think you were going to let us starve." He added, "Our radio batteries ran down last night. I hope you brought a new set."

"No worries," said MacDougall. He went on, "Had a spot of bother with the truck. That's why I'm late. Had to get a part sent up and it took longer than I expected." He opened the back of the truck and threw the tarpaulin back. The men began to unload their supplies.

"Say, Mac, this case of apples has been got at!" exclaimed the one called Alf. "There's some missing."

Laura, who had jumped down and was standing watching them, colored guiltily. She had forgotten to tell MacDougall about the apples. Now she caught his accusing eye. She confessed, "I was thirsty. I ate two. . . ."

The men looked at her, not comprehending, naturally. Laura waited for MacDougall to tell them she was a stowaway. It was bound to be good for a laugh.

However, he said, "Miss Fairchild evidently had a craving for apples. I shall have to add it to her bill."

There was mild amusement but, to Laura, even that was not funny. She had given MacDougall one more example of her irresponsibility by taking what was not hers.

Lunch was a hearty meal of canned spaghetti bolognese, soda bread made in a camp oven and more scalding hot tea. They finished off with apples, but Laura, catching MacDougall's sardonic eye, felt compelled to refuse one.

There were two other men, she learned, who were away from the camp at the moment, prospecting. The team was doing geological surveys for copper and other minerals. They had some good showings, they told MacDougall, in a few areas nearby. They would be moving on again shortly, and so for some minutes the men all pored over a map so that MacDougall would know where to find them next time.

The prospectors were intrigued when they discovered that Laura was going to see her brother who was living with one of the aboriginal tribes, but at least they were more sympathetic than MacDougall, and seemed to accept her need as quite natural, without any explanations.

After lunch they rested for a short time, MacDougall lazily smoking his pipe, and Laura with Caesar's head on her lap, a circumstance that caused Bill to comment that she must be okay if Caesar liked her, and MacDougall to look sour. Then, his pipe finished, MacDougall leapt up and said it was time to go.

Bill said, as they walked to the truck. "I wouldn't bank on making it to Margaret Springs tonight, Mac. There've been quite a few washaways and you'll probably have to detour a bit, I reckon, until they can get the graders out again."

"That bad, is it?" said MacDougall, put out. "I was hoping to get to the Springs tonight." He cast a sidelong look at Laura. "I guess you might have to forgo that shower another day." His tone clearly conveyed his contempt for her fastidiousness, and his delight in her prolonged discomfort.

She said, "Oh, it doesn't worry me."

Bill warned, "I wouldn't tackle the ridge in the dark, Mac. Alf and Joe got bogged there last week and that was before the last lot of rain. I don't fancy your chances getting out on your own." He glanced at Laura. Obviously he didn't consider she would be any help in an emergency.

"Okay, I won't chance it," said MacDougall. "I don't often drive at night anyway, not in this country. I learned my lesson that time I bent an axle in a pothole I didn't see because of the bulldust."

Laura climbed back into the truck, determined this time to stake her claim to the major share of the seat, but Caesar had an insidious way of pushing his rump down hard and slumping toward her that gradually edged her, in spite of her strong resistance, nearer to MacDougall. Occasionally the dog would glance over his shoulder at her with almost a mischievous look in his eyes, as though he too was enjoying her discomfort.

"Caesar seems to have taken a shine to you," remarked MacDougall once, and Laura was not sure whether she read surprise or displeasure in his voice.

"Quite clearly a dog of discernment," she joked, stroking the animal's head. "What breed is he?"

"We call him a kangaroo dog. He's a bitzer really. Bit of greyhound, bit of Great Dane probably, bit of goodness knows what else. He's got speed and stamina. I got him off an aborigine as a pup."

"Do you hunt kangaroos?" Laura asked.

"Not unless I need food, for him or me."

"They're so beautiful," Laura said wistfully. "I can't understand why people want to kill them. . . ."

"But scorpions aren't so beautiful," he remarked dryly, and she flinched.

She retorted boldly, "All right, I take your point. I'll try to see scorpions differently from now on, but I wouldn't kill . . . just for sport."

He nodded. "Kangaroos, unfortunately, have reached pest proportions in some areas, but farmers have only got themselves to blame. They made the favorable conditions for the kangaroo to flourish in, lush pastures and permanent water, and they stuck up a few thousand miles of dingo fence to keep the kangaroo's natural enemy out."

"What are dingoes like?" Laura asked. "I've never seen one. Are they very savage?"

"Not as savage as they're made out to be. They're the same as most animals, they kill to eat, but they put sheep fairly low on their list of favorite foods, when other game is plentiful. People are beginning to realize at last that dingoes have many times been blamed unfairly for stock killing. Feral dogs are the worst enemies of sheep—domestic pets gone wild, hunting in packs, which dingoes rarely do. Most people refuse to believe that a nice friendly domestic pet can become a wanton killer if he gets into a pack."

To Laura's surprise, MacDougall was quite talkative after

the lunch stop. She was relieved. It was unnerving traveling kilometer after kilometer with someone so uncommunicative, and worse, someone who was palpably antagonistic toward her even when he wasn't speaking. He was almost friendly, she thought, as he talked about the dingoes and kangaroos and then other animals and birds. Laura learned a great deal about the country that she had not known before.

It grew hotter as the afternoon wore on, and the sun beat down through the metal roof of the truck. The breeze through the window was not a cool one, and dust laden. Laura prickled all over with the discomfort of it. Even her cotton sun hat, squashed down hard on her head, did little to reduce the heat. Her shirt was clinging to her and her slacks felt damp. She began to think of the shower she would not be getting tonight because of the washaways.

During the afternoon they had to detour several times because the road was impassable. In one place a tangled mass of red earth and tree roots completely blocked the way for some distance, and MacDougall had to maneuver the truck through thick bush for quite some time before they could return to the road. As the truck humped and bumped over the rough terrain, Laura was unmercifully thrown about. As Caesar was next to the window, she had nothing to cling to for support, so was constantly pitched into either the dog or MacDougall. Sometimes her spine felt so jarred she wished she had never embarked on this lunatic enterprise, at others she realized that in spite of everything—the discomfort and the antagonism of MacDougall—she was enjoying herself enormously.

They had been on the road for an hour or so when MacDougall suddenly glanced at Laura and said, "Hot?"

It was the understatement of the year, she thought, but, belying her moist face, she answered, "I'm okay."

"It can get hotter than this—a lot hotter," drawled Mac-Dougall, with a certain relish, and managing to diminish her endurance.

A short while later he turned the truck off along a narrow road. After twisting and turning through the scrubby bush and around low hills and up over rocky places where the road

57

sometimes seemed to disappear altogether, MacDougall finally stopped. They were, Laura noticed, quite deep in the hills.

MacDougall said, "Get out!"

Laura obeyed, and Caesar, who seemed to recognize the spot, galloped off barking joyfully.

"Follow me," ordered MacDougall peremptorily.

Laura was wary. She had thought this was just a stop for tea or a can of beer. However, she found herself trailing after him through the bush, half curious, half nervous, and acutely aware once more of the fact that she was utterly at his mercy.

They had walked only a short distance when MacDougall turned to her and said, "How about a swim? Would that cool you down?"

"A swim!" Laura, who had been obeying his previous injunction to look where she was going in her flimsy sandals, and was still looking down, thought she must have misheard him. When she looked up, however, she saw before her a glimmering sheet of water, so clear she could see golden sand at the bottom of it. It was surrounded by much lusher vegetation than she had seen all day.

"And don't protest that you forgot your bathers," said MacDougall. "No one will see you skinny-dipping—except me and Caesar."

Laura turned a fiery red. "It looks very inviting," she murmured, walking onto the huge flat rock that overhung one end of the water hole. She longed to plunge straight in.

MacDougall regarded her teasingly. "Jump in then. I'm going to." He added, in a commanding tone, "First, though, you can wash our clothes and spread them on the rock. They'll be dry in a couple of jiffies." He began to strip off.

Laura turned her back, unsure what to do. As she stood there hesitantly, he laughed at her. "What's the matter? Modest, are you? You needn't worry. I've seen girls without their clothes on before. It won't upset me! But if you want to be prim, you can leave your underwear on!" Next moment Laura heard a splash as his body hit the water.

She wanted to shout something very rude at him, but she couldn't think of anything. So, she stripped off her shirt and slacks, then hesitated again. She could not quite bring herself to go swimming in the nude with this stranger. She would be embarrassed, even if he wasn't. Let him laugh at her, if he wanted, she didn't care, she thought.

Nettled by the curt way he had ordered her to do the washing, she nevertheless meekly complied, mindful of the fact that she was with him under sufferance and that obedience might make him more kindly disposed toward her.

She dumped their clothes in the water and called out, "Have you got any soap?"

He swam to where she was standing near the edge and she noticed he was still wearing his underpants. In deference to her?

"Soap?" he echoed, with disgust. "Soap would foul the water. Haven't you any sense at all?" He turned and swam away from her and she silently clenched her fists and shook them after him, at the same time angry with herself for making such a blunder.

"I bet a little bit of soap wouldn't hurt," she muttered to herself, sure that he was using any excuse to belittle her.

Vigorously she doused the clothes up and down in the water, which colored red from the dust out of both their gear. When they were as clean as she could get them, she scrambled back to the rock and laid them out to dry in the hot sun. MacDougall was languorously swimming the length of the water hole, his deeply tanned body glistening as he scythed through the water with powerful strokes of his muscular arms and legs.

Laura watched with a feeling of helpless chagrin. No doubt he was enjoying the fact that she had obeyed his command like some submissive peasant wife. She wished now she had told him to wash his own clothes, but it was too late.

She dived into the water. Its cool depths closed over her with a delicious tingling, almost taking her breath away. The relief of it was wonderful. When she surfaced, she found MacDougall near her, his wet hair clinging around his face, and his heavily lashed gray eyes mocking her, as they took in the fact that she was still clad in her underwear.

"I didn't expect such a bold young lady as you to be so

modest!" he teased. Swimming seemed to have relaxed him, and he was less abrasive now, almost friendly in fact.

"Maybe I'm not as bold as you like to think," Laura countered, holding his gaze, although the memory of last night remained with skin-tingling clarity, and she was wary of him.

"Perhaps bold isn't quite the right word," he murmured. "Perhaps enterprising suits you better."

Laura was not sure she cared for that description either. If he meant it in the connection she thought he did, it suggested she was some sort of scheming female. Not anxious to pursue a discussion along those lines, she struck out strongly across the water hole away from him, not stopping until she had almost reached the other side.

As she turned, he yelled out, "Watch out for crocodiles!"

"What!" She almost leapt out of the water, and immediately began to swim frantically back toward him.

Then she saw that he was convulsed with laughter. "I was only joking!" he spluttered. "There aren't any here!"

"Mean beast!" exclaimed Laura, annoyed with herself for being taken in and letting him take advantage of her ignorance. She lunged at him, splashing violently for a moment or two, and then swam swiftly away from him. She turned on her back and floated with her face upturned to the sky, feeling totally relaxed now, and curiously happy.

A moment later MacDougall was beside her. He grasped her ankle and tugged playfully at it. "Where did you learn to swim so well?"

"Oh, on long lazy holidays in Cannes and Nice and Juan-les-Pins . . ." she lied flippantly. She wrenched her foot free of his grasp and trod water as she shot him an impudent look. "Isn't that what you expected?"

He swam up close to her and looked steadily into her eyes. "You're a lousy liar," he said, and his eyes twinkled with unexpected amusement.

Laura kicked away from him, retorting. "Well, would you believe Bournemouth, then, an unwilling maiden aunt on whom I was foisted, and there was nothing else to do?"

SAVAGE MOON

A short burst of laughter escaped him. "No! That sounds equally as bizarre."

She rolled over and struck out across the water hole again. "Well, it's true. Come on, race you back to the rocks!"

A shower of spray told her he had passed her, but she swam on, determined not to be far behind. When he turned near the rocks where she had laid their clothes out to dry, she did not notice and swam right into his outstretched arms. They both sank, arms and legs entangled, and surfaced laughing into each other's shoulders. Briefly their eyes met in an unguarded look, and Laura knew a moment of panic as it seemed that his slightly parted lips were about to meet her own. She knew she would never be able to resist the kiss if that was what he intended, but knowing he only mocked her, she would feel humiliated. So, with an effort of will she promptly ducked him, which led to his retaliation, and they engaged in some minutes of vigorous horseplay, their laughter echoing across the still, empty bush.

Eventually Laura, exhilarated but breathless, cried out, "Enough! Stop!" She swam from him and trod water breathlessly at a distance, laughter still bubbling out of her. She was glad she had defused what might have been a regretted moment for both of them. In spite of it she still felt a marvelous sense of well-being, which seemed to flow through every part of her down to her fingertips and toes. She stretched out to float on her back again, exhausted, but happy.

MacDougall's long brown body knifed through the water and he floated alongside her. They gazed at the cloudless blue sky in silence. The heat of the sun was beginning to diminish with the advancing afternoon, and its rays slanted through the trees, making a dappled pattern on the water. Laura moved only her fingers and toes in delicious appreciation of the silky cool water, but was tinglingly conscious of the man beside her, especially when his fingers brushed across her upturned palm, and when his thigh accidentally touched hers.

"You're a funny girl," he murmured reflectively after a time.

61

Laura stiffened warily, wondering what the remark signified, if he was about to deride her again.

"I'm glad I make you laugh," she returned dryly.

When no further remarks were forthcoming from him, she
turned her head surreptitiously to study his profile, upturned
to the sky. It was a strong profile, but seemed softer now that
he was completely relaxed, and although she would have
given a great deal to know what he was thinking, she did not
let it bother her too much. She felt so utterly at peace, with
the world, with herself, even with MacDougall. . . .

At last he seemed to sense her scrutiny and turned his head
toward her. His gray eyes were speculative, and he seemed
about to say something, then changed his mind. Perhaps it
was wishful thinking again, but for a moment Laura was sure
there had been a softer look in his eyes, as though some
barrier had suddenly been lifted.

It was short-lived. Before she could even rejoice, the blank
wall was back again, as though he had become aware of his
lapse and was annoyed with himself, and in an instant he had
withdrawn from her both physically and mentally.

He said in a gritty tone, "I'm going out."

The interlude of pure bliss was shattered. Laura felt the
pleasure of the past few minutes wrenched away from her as
she heard him splash his way to the rocks and felt the ripples
he made wash over her. She did not follow. The water
returned to its glassy smoothness after he had gone, and she
floated languidly, feeling somehow cheated.

"Laura!" It was the first time he had used her first name,
and the call startled her. How long it had been since he had
left her she did not know. She trod water and looked around
for him. He was standing on the big rock, tall and tanned—
like some proud savage, she thought romantically, immediately chiding herself for such a wayward fantasy. But, looking
up at him, she knew suddenly something that was not fantasy.
Since meeting MacDougall, life had changed dramatically.
Nothing looked quite the same anymore, and in some subtle
way even she had altered. It was a feeling without foundation,
just a simple intuition, but it was strong enough to be a little
unnerving. Something was happening to her, something

inexorable, although she scarcely recognized what it was yet. She only knew she must fight it.

She swam to the rock. He looked down at her, saying brusquely, "Tea's made." He was wearing only his trousers and the hairs on his broad bare chest still glistened with droplets of water. He turned and walked back toward the truck, not even offering to assist her to climb out of the water. Laura, for some strange reason, felt abandoned.

She heaved herself up onto the rock and sat there dripping for a moment or two. The sun began to dry her almost at once. Her shirt and slacks were bone dry, but she did not want to put them on over wet underwear, nor did she want to stay as she was now she was out of the water. So, hiding behind a bush, she stripped off her underwear and quickly pulled on her shirt and slacks. Then she draped her bra and panties over the bush to dry, before she went to join MacDougall.

"Feeling better?" he inquired, surveying her with a guarded, but nevertheless quite friendly look.

"Marvelous," she enthused. "This is a superb spot. Out of this world. How did you ever find it?"

"If you travel in dry country," he answered, "you need to know where to find water. The aborigines know where all the water holes are. That's how they managed to survive for thousands of years before white men came. What's more, they always lived in total harmony with the land, taking only what they needed, never despoiling, never upsetting the delicate balance of nature."

"You sound as though you admire them very much."

He treated her to a crushing look. "Why not? In many ways they know a lot more about living than we do. Not the ones that hang around the towns and settlements. We've succeeded in making many of them forget the real meaning of life, unfortunately, but there are still some left who have not entirely adopted white man's foolish ways. You'll meet some when we find Eric and the tribe."

He poured tea into their two mugs.

"You talk almost as though he is one of them," said Laura, intrigued.

"He is. He was fully initiated, an honor not given to many white men. He respected them, and they showed their acceptance of him in the only possible way. They made him a full blood brother." He glanced at her, a sidelong disparaging glance. "Somehow I don't see you as their full blood sister."

"You do love to tilt at me, don't you?" she complained, nettled again.

He made no apology, but stood up and said, "Bring your tea down to the rock."

She picked up her mug and he carried the tin kettle and his own mug down to the large flat rock beside the water hole. Before he sat down he dug something out of his pocket which Laura saw was a length of fishing line, and a hook with a grub attached. He flung the line out across the mirror surface of the pond. The ripples spread for a moment and then the stillness returned.

It was very peaceful lazing beside the water hole. In spite of her edginess with MacDougall, Laura felt utterly relaxed. She felt she could stay forever just idly watching the dragonflies skimming the water, the tiny lizards that scuttled across the warm rocks or basked on the edges of them, motionless, beady dark eyes watching warily, and just listening to the muted sounds of cicadas in some distant trees, the intermittent fluting calls of a bird.

At last she said, "Do you have a first name?" He had used hers, a gesture of friendliness, she thought, suggesting he might be thawing a little toward her in spite of his sometimes still scratchy manner. She felt she had a right to use his if he could use hers. She added, "Mr. MacDougall sounds so formal."

He chuckled softly. "I hadn't noticed! As a matter of fact I seldom do enjoy that formality. Most people call me either MacDougall or Mac."

"Well, what shall I call you?" Laura persisted after this rather unsatisfactory answer. "You apparently don't object to first names since you used mine a few minutes ago."

His eyes glinted at her. "Did I take a liberty? I beg your pardon, but as I recall, you did invite me to."

She knew he was laughing at her so she resisted the temptation to bite. Eventually he decided to enlighten her.

"My first name is Robert." He said it almost with embarrassment, and then added quickly, and most emphatically, "But no one has called me that for years. It's either MacDougall or Mac. Take your pick. I answer to both." Implicit in his tone was the warning that although he had not forbidden it, he would not welcome her using his first name. That, she thought dismally, would be putting their relationship on too personal a basis, which he was clearly at pains to avoid. MacDougall was not a man to allow anyone too close to him. But it could be even more than that, she reflected, stealing a glance at his granite profile; it was almost as though by being just MacDougall he was hiding his more personal, perhaps more vulnerable, self even from himself.

It suited him anyway, she thought, the terse single name. It suited his arrogance, his self-sufficient image, his aloofness. It conjured up visions of a Scottish laird, proud as the stag he hunted, gaunt as his highland hills, tough as the rocky paths he trod. Although this was Australia, not Scotland, the image was the same, of a man at one with his environment, an intrinsic part of it, yet always in control. A man others would know without question, a man you would not cross if you could help it.

Laura said meekly, "I'll call you Mac if I may."

"Suit yourself," he said with infuriating indifference.

There was a tug on his line and he started forward with an exclamation of satisfaction, and began hauling in the fish. A medium-sized silver fish wriggled on the hook. MacDougall swiftly beheaded it with his knife.

"That'll do nicely for our supper," he said. "I hope you know what to do with a fish that isn't ready filleted, frozen and crumbed." He could never resist an opportunity to have a go at her, she thought.

"Of course," Laura answered promptly, adding sarcastically. "You would believe a finishing school and cordon bleu, naturally!" As it happened, it was true.

He laughed, made no comment but called to the dog. "Caesar! Fish head!"

Caesar had wandered away and did not appear immediately, which caused MacDougall to call again, more sharply, "Caesar! Here, boy!"

There was a movement in the bushes near where Laura had spread her underwear, and next moment Caesar emerged, rather sheepishly, something white dangling from his muzzle. Laura gasped. Her eyes flew to the bush, and back to the mangled piece of white cloth in the dog's jaws.

She leapt up shrieking, "My bra! Oh, no! You wicked dog!" She scrambled toward him, snatching at the scrap of material. "You bad, bad dog, you've chewed up my bra!" Caesar thought she wanted a game, and he tugged vigorously, as she tried to wrest the garment from him. "Let go . . . let go, you horrible animal!" she cried, giving an extra sharp tug. There was a sudden sound of tearing material, and Laura overbalanced and fell back on top of the still partially recumbent MacDougall, a small scrap of white cotton in her fingers.

His arms folded around her waist as she toppled into his lap, and he held her tightly, as he rocked with a surge of spontaneous laughter, his face pressed against her neck. For a moment she wanted to explode with fury, but his overwhelming nearness banished every other feeling but the rush of involuntary pleasure it gave her.

Chapter Five

It was idiotic to feel so embarrassed about it, Laura told herself over and over, but it made no difference. It was almost worse than being naked, she thought, especially as MacDougall regarded it as a huge joke, and every time she caught his eye, which to her always seemed to be fixed on the opening of her shirt, he smiled mockingly, hugely enjoying her new discomfort.

To add to her dismay, she had lost the top button of her shirt which had burst off when she fell back into MacDougall's arms during the tug-of-war with Caesar. She was now particularly conscious of her revealing neckline as she was bending over the fire to cook the fish. The job required her full attention, and she was nervous because she knew MacDougall was watching, hoping no doubt to find fault.

At first she had not realized how clearly visible to him were the firm curving contours of her breasts, freed from the restrictions of a brassiere. When she did, her hand flew swiftly to her throat, to clutch the edges of her shirt together. Involuntarily, she glanced at him, and saw him laughing silently.

"I don't know why you're so touchy," he said, in a dry tone. "I thought bras were out of date anyway." He cocked his head quizzically at her. "Though I don't see you as one of the bra-burning brigade."

"No, I was not," she answered irritably. She slapped his piece of fish onto the tin plate alongside the potato she had baked in the coals, and handed it to him. "I hope it's to your liking," she said, a trifle sarcastically.

"It looks and smells delicious." He lifted the plate to his nose and sniffed appreciatively.

"Do you want your tea now?" Laura asked, annoyed with him, and yet feeling something else as well, a feeling she was angry about and determined to suppress. It was ridiculous, but it had caught her unawares this afternoon, and now she could not help remembering all the time, the strong warm contact of his hands on her bare waist when she had tumbled over and he had caught her in his arms and held her tightly. The feeling disturbed her greatly. It was all wrong to have that sort of feeling for a man you disliked, and who treated you as no better than the sole of his boot and whose chief delight was to mock and deride.

"I said yes, thanks," MacDougall repeated, and Laura realized she had been miles away. Her hand trembled as she poured, and was still shaking as she handed the mug to him. When she had poured her own mug of tea, she set the kettle back on the fire and inadvertently brushed the edge of her palm across the hot metal.

"Ouch!" she exclaimed involuntarily, dragging it quickly away and raising the burn instinctively to her mouth.

MacDougall glanced up. "What's up?"

"Nothing." She lowered her hand and began to eat from the frying pan. The burn began to throb.

"You burned yourself," MacDougall said.

"It's nothing much."

"Leave some tea in the kettle," he advised. "Cold tea is good for burns. Takes the sting out."

"Thanks," she said, "but it's not that bad."

After they had eaten, they sat on either side of the fire and there was a strangely domestic coziness about it, Laura mused, in spite of the wild bush surroundings, the rough-and-ready meal. There was even a kind of companionship despite the way they struck sparks off each other. One minute she was regretting her acquiescence in washing his clothes and cooking his meal, because she was sure that was all he believed women were good for, and the next she had the craziest notion that she would enjoy doing just that for the rest of her life.

Caesar spread himself out close to the fire, occasionally raising his head to look at one or the other of them as though checking to see if they were still there. There was silence for some time until finally MacDougall said:

"I'm sorry Caesar chewed up your bra, Laura, and I'm sorry I laughed. That was unkind, but if you could have seen your face . . . ! Frankly, it was the funniest thing I've seen in a long time." He chuckled, and his eyes twinkled merrily in the firelight.

Suddenly Laura forgave him. She forgave him his casual treatment of her, his roughness, his mockery. She began to laugh also. "I can see the funny side of it now, too, but I was so mad with him at the time." She giggled. "It was my fault, I suppose. I should have kept an eye on my things."

"A pity you departed in too much of a hurry to bring a change of clothing," MacDougall remarked dryly.

Laura bridled. "I wouldn't have had to leave so precipitately if you . . ." She stopped, not wanting to start an argument when the atmosphere was suddenly more relaxed.

MacDougall said, "Unfortunately, although I carry a change of gear, I don't have anything remotely resembling a brassiere!" He grinned at her teasingly. "I'm afraid you'll have to suffer being a liberated woman for the rest of the trip."

Laura had a sudden thought. "What about Margaret Springs? Are there any women there? I might be able to—"

MacDougall threw back his head and laughed again. "There's a woman at Margaret Springs all right, but Mrs. Gordon is fifteen stone and somewhat on the buxom side." He eyed Laura speculatively, observing the way her shirt stretched tautly across her breasts. "Without disparaging

69

your quite delightful contours, I would reckon anything she could lend you would be several sizes too large."

Laura blushed and changed the subject. "More tea?"

He held out his mug. "Thanks."

It was strange, Laura thought, as she refilled it, that in the last few minutes something had changed subtly in their relationship—and it was for the better. Some kind of barrier was down, she felt sure, or was it just that her own softening toward him was making her indulge in wishful thinking?

"You must lead a rather lonely sort of life," she ventured after another silence. His apparent preference for his own company puzzled her.

"Suits me," he answered shortly, and then, narrowing his gaze, warned sharply, "so don't get any ideas about changing me."

Laura bit her lip. She was always saying the wrong things.

"It hadn't occurred to me to try," she retorted. "I'm only interested in finding my brother."

"And then back to the fleshpots of London . . ."

Laura laughed. "Fleshpots! How old fashioned and square can you get!" She enjoyed the opportunity to mock him for a change. It provided a cover for her real feelings at the moment. It would never do for this man to suspect how strongly she was attracted to him. She must show her indifference in every way possible.

He ignored the jibe and asked, "I suppose you enjoy working in a beauty parlor?"

The question startled her. She had never really considered it before. She had just worked at her job. Suddenly, faced with qualifying it, she hesitated. Did she enjoy it? She was not sure all at once. All those brittle, spoiled women seeking to prolong their good looks or to manufacture looks they did not have, the cruel gossip she often overheard, the patronizing way some of them treated her—suddenly she was filled with a revulsion that she realized had always been there, but had never been acknowledged. So what had made her change? She glanced at MacDougall. She knew it was he. In a very brief time, he had made her begin to question her whole existence.

She took a deep breath. "Yes, I enjoy it," and knew for the first time that it was a lie. But she must not let him guess that.

He had an image of her which she must be careful to maintain. It was the only way she was going to get out of this without emotional scars.

He made no further comment, but remarked, "I want to get away early tomorrow, so we'd better turn in."

Laura crawled into her sleeping bag and once more stretched out on the ground on the opposite side of the truck from MacDougall, protesting when he had again suggested she sleep in the truck, that she preferred the ground.

"Stubborn little pom, aren't you?" he chided, but for once there was no sarcasm in the jibe. Laura did not answer.

She lay awake for some time looking at the stars, marveling at their profusion and brilliance. Like the lights of some vast metropolis in the sky, she mused to herself, and we're on a spaceship homing in to the airport. . . .

She drifted off into a deep sleep almost at once. Only moments later she woke with a start, knowing something had startled her, but unable to recall what. And then, from far away, came a long mournful howl. She knew it must be a dingo. She sat up, listening, and through the trees on a distant ridge saw the moon rising. It was almost full and hung huge and blood-red against the blue-black sky. The dingo howled again and a strange feeling crept over her, as though the present had ceased to be, and she stood at the beginning of time.

As she watched the moon rise, a shadow suddenly came between her and it. MacDougall stood a few paces away, looking toward her, not speaking, his face a featureless shadow. As the moon rose slowly behind him, he seemed to loom larger and larger and more forbidding, like one of the aboriginal dreamtime spirits he had told her about earlier in a rare burst of talkativeness as they sat by the fire.

Laura closed her eyes, and when she opened them again, he had gone. Perhaps she had only dreamed he was there. The moon was golden now, and drifting behind a veil of cloud. The dingo did not howl again, and Laura sank back into a troubled sleep.

71

It was not, however, of the ghostly figure of MacDougall that she dreamed, but of Romilly. He came to her London flat as though nothing had happened, as though they could carry on as before, in spite of his faithlessness. He was angry when she told him they could not. He ranted and raved like a spoiled child, then cajoled and wheedled and tried to win her over. When she accused him of only wanting her money, he was outraged, then abject. But she would not take him back. She shouted it at him, told him to go and leave her alone, but he would not. His features hardened and his eyes glowed menacingly as he came toward her.

"Romilly, leave me . . . please . . ." she cried. "I don't love you."

"We'll see about that," he answered coarsely, confident of his power over her.

She stepped back and found herself hard against a wall, trapped.

"No!"

He advanced, grabbed her and tried to push her down onto a couch. She struggled violently, lashing out at him with her knees, her head, her hands, as she desperately tried to escape and she screamed . . . and screamed . . . and screamed . . .

Then the nightmare stopped, but she was still being shaken furiously.

"Laura! Laura!"

With a shock she woke to find herself held in an iron grip just as in the nightmare, except that it was MacDougall's fingers digging into her flesh, his face looming close to hers. In real panic this time, she began to struggle, the nightmare forgotten as the reality filled her with horror.

"Get away from me, you brute . . . get away from me. . . ." He held her fast and all she could do was scream.

"Pull yourself together!" he commanded her roughly, and smartly slapped her face.

The shock made her stop struggling. "How dare you!" she breathed, half angry, half terrified. "How dare you!"

He released her none too gently. "You're hysterical," he said calmly.

"Well, who wouldn't be, waking up to find themselves

being violently assaulted." She eyed him warily, her heart pounding. The moonlight was silver and cold, and the bush utterly still. Laura could see his face clearly. Cold anger was there.

"I was not assaulting you," he said in a level tone. "You screamed out in your sleep, and I came to see what was the matter. I imagine you were having some kind of nightmare." He drew a deep breath. "Perhaps in your dream you imagined . . ."

She remembered and was ashamed of her hysterics. "I'm sorry . . . it was a nightmare . . . and it wasn't you. . . ."

"I suppose I should be grateful for that," he commented dryly.

She couldn't help it then, she began to cry. She knew he would despise her weakness or even think she was doing it on purpose to gain his sympathy. She expected him to say something cutting about women and tears, but she could not help herself. The tears flowed.

It was a huge relief. She had not realized before how great the tension inside her had been since her mother's death, Romilly's defection, and the emptiness had begun to stretch so interminably in front of her. She was no longer proof against it. Her defenses were down completely. Let him mock, she thought weakly, what do I care?

But to her immense surprise, he did not mock. In a moment he was beside her, his arm around her shoulders, holding her against him, awkward though it was with her still trussed in the sleeping bag. His hard hands smoothed her face and hair soothingly, and although he did not speak, she sensed sympathy which was so unexpected that it moved her unbearably and caused fresh tears to flow. He pushed a handkerchief into her hand.

It would have been better had he been rough and mocking, she thought. He was treating her like a little girl, a child who is overwrought, frightened by bogeymen in the night, and bitterly she realized that she did not want him to think of her like that. In spite of everything, she wanted him to treat her like a woman.

Her head lay against his chest and she could feel the

rhythmic pounding of his heart against her cheek. It was soothing and eventually she fell asleep, not realizing it. When she woke it was still dark, although there were faint chinks of light in the eastern sky above the ranges. The stars were cold and distant and low down lay the Southern Cross, tilted to the pole. For a moment Laura did not realize that she was still half sitting, and that she was leaning not against the truck but against MacDougall. He was propped against the wheel of the truck, one gray blanket very inadequately tucked around him. His head rested against the top of hers, and he was sound asleep.

Why hadn't he left her hours ago? He couldn't have meant to stay with her, surely. In a rush, the previous night came back to her and her cheeks flooded with shame. What a spectacle she had made of herself.

Even as the thought entered her mind, MacDougall stirred. Instinctively Laura closed her eyes again and pretended to be still asleep. She was sure he would be chagrined to find he had fallen asleep in such a position, and would prefer that she was unaware she had slept with her head pillowed on his chest. That would suggest a softness he did not own to. That he had stayed with her, out of consideration for her, was a possibility she hardly dared contemplate, as it seemed so unlikely.

He moved so gently and quietly that, with her eyes shut tight, she was scarcely aware of being lowered to the ground and the rolled blanket tucked under her head. How stiff and cold he must be, she thought guiltily. He had had only the thin blanket covering him all night. And how he must despise her for her weakness. Yet he had comforted her, she remembered. He had held her against him and soothed her like a child . . . but that was only how he thought of her, a spoiled child.

There was silence, and Laura imagined he must have stolen away very quietly so as not to waken her. She was about to open her eyes when something touched her lips, so lightly she was not even sure a moment afterward that it had happened, but there was the faint aroma of pipe tobacco to confirm it—MacDougall had kissed her!

A moment later she heard his light footfall as he walked

away but she did not open her eyes for some minutes. She was too bemused. He had kissed her! Just a light brushing of his lips across hers but a kiss nonetheless. She was perplexed. Hadn't he said quite categorically he would never do so again?

She felt too agitated to remain where she was for much longer. It was growing lighter and there was a blush of crimson over the hills. A bird, which she now recognized as a pied butcher-bird, warbled melodiously nearby, and Caesar barked briefly. Laura wriggled out of her sleeping bag. The air was cool but not cold. She pulled on her cardigan and, hearing sounds near the campfire, went to join MacDougall. She felt embarrassed and rather shamefaced. How would he treat her this morning, this enigmatic man?

He looked up as she approached. "'Morning," he greeted her gruffly, and went back to poking the fire into life.

"Good morning," Laura said, standing watching, searching for something appropriate to say. At last she muttered, "Sorry I disturbed you last night."

He glanced at her sharply, and she knew he was seeking some sign that she was aware how he had spent the night. He said slowly, "Nightmares aren't pleasant. Yours was particularly nasty, judging by the power of your screams. I hope you slept better afterwards."

"Yes, thank you, I did," Laura answered. "I'm very sorry—"

"Stop saying you're sorry and make yourself useful," he commanded brusquely. "Go and fill the kettle." There was no discernible change in his tone or attitude toward her.

Laura picked up the kettle and walked down to the water hole. Caesar followed her, walking demurely at her side as though to guard her. She ruffled his head affectionately, and was careful to look where she was going, just in case she encountered a scorpion or worse along the path.

"Good dog," she murmured, but as they approached the water hole, Caesar's hackles suddenly rose and he stopped, his ears cocked, staring into the bush. A couple of colorful parrots abruptly fled from a tree beside the water hole, but this was not what concerned Caesar. Laura paused, and instinctively gripped the dog's collar. They both watched as several big gray kangaroos hopped down to the water's edge to drink.

Caesar tugged on his collar but Laura held him back. One kangaroo, catching their scent, lifted its head, ears pricked, and stared straight at them. Immediately the others looked up too, and for a moment all stood on their great hind legs, front paws dangling before them, staring at Laura and the dog. One had a joey peering out of its pouch. Then, as though at a silent command, they all turned and bounded off through the bush with a loud thumping of their powerful tails. Laura thought she had never seen anything so graceful, or so beautiful.

Caesar pulled impatiently, almost dragging her along with him, but she scolded severely, "Leave them be, Caesar!" She kept a firm hold of his collar until they reached the water's edge, by which time he had found other things to interest him and was eagerly snuffling after real or imaginary quarries in the bushes.

Laura leaned over the rock and filled the kettle with the cold sparkling water. Then she splashed her face vigorously and felt immensely refreshed. She noticed there was now a large blister where she had burned her hand but it was no longer as painful. When she returned to the camp the fire was burning merrily, and MacDougall was frying sausages, turning them in the pan with a stick. He glanced up.

"What kept you?" he demanded irritably.

Laura placed the kettle of water on the fire and gave him a swift look. She knew he was bitterly regretting his lapse into chivalry last night, and in case she had any wrong ideas about his softness, he was making sure they were quickly eliminated.

"Kangaroos," she told him, with spontaneous enthusiasm. "Six of them . . . oh, Mac, they were so beautiful. They all stood up and looked at us with their soft dark eyes, and those little front paws dangling, so surprised! And one had a baby in its pouch!"

Fleetingly, a faint smile curved his lips and there was a brief softening of his expression, but it quickly faded.

He said, "I heard something. I thought it might be 'roos."

"They were the first I've ever seen," she said, still enthralled by the memory of the scene that had been so fleeting, yet which she knew would stay with her always. She looked around and heaved a happy sigh. "I love . . . all this . . . the bush. I never thought I would, but it's so . . . so . . ." She stopped, shrugged, feeling embarrassed. "I don't know," she finished lamely, "I just can't explain it."

"Don't go getting all sentimental just because you saw a bunch of 'roos," said MacDougall abrasively. "Here, take over the grub."

They breakfasted quickly and in almost total silence. Laura ran down to the water hole afterward to wash up the plates and mugs, and at the same time clean her teeth and have a wash. She would have liked to linger in this idyllic spot but knew MacDougall was impatient to be off. A short while later, before the sun was quite up, they were on their way. Laura looked back at the water hole with a pang of regret. She felt she had experienced something close to real happiness there, and yet also, she reflected ruefully, something painful too.

MacDougall, not unexpectedly, was grim-faced and even more taciturn than usual. Laura supposed he was probably also rather tired after spending most of the night in a cramped position. He did not refer to it, however, and she gave no hint that she knew she had not been alone all night. She was disappointed, though, because the incident had spoiled what she had hoped was a change for the better in their relationship.

She concentrated on the scenery instead of the man beside her, but it was hard not to be aware of his large frame next to her, his big rough hands gripping the steering wheel, his battered hat pushed back on his head, revealing his broad brow, craggy unshaven profile and the grim line of his mouth. As before, she was thrown this way and that by the rough road, and although he was probably unconscious of it, she was acutely aware of his arm sometimes brushing her breast through her thin shirt, and it disconcerted her.

There was plenty to distract her, but even flocks of brightly colored parrots and kangaroos that bounded across in front of them were not enough to keep her thoughts permanently away from MacDougall. The going was, in places, even rougher than yesterday, and sometimes the truck almost stopped in soft soil where there had been a washaway, and Laura was sure they would never make it, but eventually it would rumble and jolt onto the road again. MacDougall would change gears and curse softly under his breath, sometimes, it seemed, having quite forgotten Laura was even there.

He spoke little, except to identify the birds that flew in front of them, or to answer when Laura asked the name of a flowering bush. She gasped in amazement when they came upon hillsides covered with a low-growing crimson flowering plant that made the red earth glow even more richly and the hills look as though they were flowing with blood.

"Wild hops," MacDougall told her. "Or rosy dock, as some people call it. The Afghans brought the seeds as ballast in their saddlebags on their camels, and gradually it's spread all through the inland."

"It's so vivid," said Laura, longing to stop and look at the flowers more closely, but not daring to ask him for fear of a sharp rebuke. Instead she remarked, "I wondered how Camel Creek got its name."

MacDougall swerved suddenly to avoid a pothole and Laura was flung hard against him. He said, "There aren't many Afghans left now, but there are plenty of feral camels in some places."

They reached Margaret Springs, another isolated station, by lunchtime. They had left the ranges behind and crossed another stretch of flat featureless country to reach the homestead. It was an old mud brick house with a corrugated-iron roof, and there were two or three big trees sheltering it, a collection of corrugated-iron buildings a short distance away from it, and beyond it all an interminably flat plain, featureless except for one or two hills that stuck up, Laura thought, like warts on weathered skin, and the fringe of distant ranges which they had come from.

"It's so desolate," Laura breathed, as they drove up. She

wondered again how anyone could bear to live in such an isolated place and how, indeed, they could make a living. She couldn't even see an animal, although MacDougall had told her the Gordons raised cattle.

Mrs. Gordon came out to meet them just as soon as the truck stopped, with a swirl of dust, in front of the house. Her hands were floury. She was in the middle of making bread, she said, and had not stopped to wipe them, so eager was she to greet the visitors. She did not notice Laura at first. She embraced MacDougall in a motherly fashion and he took off his hat and slapped her ample bottom with it.

"Hiya, Mrs. Gordon," he said in a jovial tone that Laura had not had the pleasure of hearing before. It was certainly not a tone he used with her. "How's things?"

"Can't grumble," said the woman cheerfully. "Joe's around somewhere. I'll give him a hoy." She picked up a stick and banged loudly on an old kerosene can suspended from a post. A deafening clatter shattered the silence. Then she spotted Laura, who had jumped down from the truck and was standing a little apart.

"Mac . . . you didn't say you'd brought a visitor," she reproached. She crossed quickly to Laura, who was aware of a rapid and very thorough scrutiny from darting blue eyes. "Welcome, my dear," said Mrs. Gordon warmly. She turned and shot a questioning glance at MacDougall.

He explained briefly why Laura was there. Mrs. Gordon seemed surprised. "Well, well, Professor Fairchild's sister, are you? You've come a long way to see your brother. I don't know how you managed to persuade Mac to bring you. He won't take passengers as a rule." She shot MacDougall a smiling look but he remained impassive. She went on, "You must be having a really rough ride. The roads are in an appalling state since the rains." She glanced at MacDougall again, "We guessed that was what must be delaying you."

He shook his head and explained about the part for the truck. Then Joe Gordon appeared and shook hands with MacDougall. He greeted Laura with a look of curiosity. Her presence was quickly explained to him, and then Mrs. Gordon bustled them all inside the house. Lunch, she said, would be ready just as soon as she'd put her batch of bread in the oven. Meanwhile they could have a beer and a shower.

Laura declined the beer, but was grateful for the shower. She did not mention the loss of her bra to Mrs. Gordon as it was obvious, as MacDougall had said, that she was unlikely to have anything suitable to lend her. In any case, explanations would involve telling how she came to be with MacDougall without any spare clothes. Laura luxuriated in the warm shower as long as she dared, enjoyed toweling herself on the big soft towel Mrs. Gordon had left for her and then examined her face in the bedroom mirror after she had dressed.

She had not been out in the sun very much but already there was a suggestion of a tan creeping into her pale skin. Her hair felt softer after shampooing, and when she had smoothed some moisturizer into her skin, she began to feel quite civilized again. She took out her compact and lipstick, thinking she would do up her face a bit, but then put them away again, not because MacDougall might sneer, but because suddenly she didn't want to bother. It was not that she would never use makeup again; it was just that it seemed incongruous in the present circumstances. As she stared at her unadorned reflection she suddenly knew what she wanted to do.

She did not want to go back to her old job in the beauty salon. She wanted to stay and help Eric. Yes, that was what she would do, she thought excitedly, she would stay and help him with his work. Immediately, she felt cheered. Even MacDougall would approve of that. He couldn't sneer at her for wanting to do that.

As a result of her inspired decision, Laura felt quite lighthearted when she joined the others for lunch. It was a lively meal, with the Gordons very reluctant to part with their guests when MacDougall said it was time they were on their way. He lingered only long enough to enjoy a quick shower himself. While he was in the bathroom, Laura helped Mrs. Gordon wash up and chatted with her. The station owner's wife was eager to know all about Laura, her life in London, and why she had come to Australia. Laura found her easy to talk to and a sympathetic listener.

"You must find it very lonely so far from civilization," Laura remarked.

Madge Gordon smiled a little ruefully. "Yes, sometimes I do, but it's not as bad as it seems. The boys—that's our sons, Jack and Warren—they have stations not too far away, and our grandchildren come to stay. Then there are regular visitors like Mac." She smiled at Laura. "He's a bit of a dark horse, isn't he?"

"He's a very private man," agreed Laura.

"He needs to get married again," declared Madge firmly.

"Again . . ." Laura was taken aback.

Madge nodded. "Don't you know? Oh, well, the less I say the better. Mac will tell you what he wants you to know. I don't want to stick my oar in. I don't know much about him anyway." She looked Laura over appraisingly. "It's not an easy life," she said. "You need to be sure you can take it. Mac'd need to be very sure, too."

"And what would I need to be sure of?"

Laura turned, startled to see him framed in the doorway, his hair still wet from the shower, clean-shaven again. How much had he overheard? Only those last few words, she hoped. He was smiling, at Mrs. Gordon, not at her. Suddenly her heart ached and she looked away. MacDougall would never consider her as a wife, no, never in a thousand years, so she had better not even think of it. Mrs. Gordon immediately chattered on and his question was left unanswered.

Loaded with samples of Mrs. Gordon's baking, including fresh loaves still warm from the oven, they eventually dragged themselves away. As they rattled down the road toward the station gate, MacDougall said, "Joe Gordon said the road's bound to be pretty bad farther on, so we won't be making any better time than we did yesterday or this morning. He's not sure how bad, unfortunately, so we'll have to keep our fingers crossed. With luck we might still meet up with the Prof tomorrow."

That was all he said for a long time, and Laura did not try

81

to engage him in conversation after her first couple of remarks about how nice the Gordons were had received monosyllabic answers. MacDougall seemed even more preoccupied than ever.

Laura dozed a little, only to be wakened with every jolt as the truck went over bumps or into potholes. Late in the afternoon they were back in the ranges again and thankfully, for some time, the road was comparatively good. The sun was low when Laura, who had briefly dozed off again, was suddenly rudely aroused by a loud curse from MacDougall.

She surfaced to find they had stopped. She looked at MacDougall questioningly, then in alarm as she saw his expression. His jaws were clenched, and he was leaning out of the window, looking down. The engine revved but the truck did not move.

"What's the matter?" Laura asked anxiously.

He turned briefly to look at her. "We're bogged," he said. "Stuck!"

Chapter Six

For a moment what he had said did not sink into Laura's mind, and even when it did, she did not at once fully appreciate the gravity of his statement.

MacDougall said, "You and Caesar get out. I'll see if less weight makes any difference." A faintly quirky smile crossed his weather-tanned face in spite of the grim situation. "Not that either of you will make a lot of difference. You both have greyhound ancestry, I reckon!"

Laura smiled weakly. It was an odd moment to make a joke. She leaned across and opened the passenger door. "Come on, Caesar, out we go," she said.

Caesar needed no persuading. He was always ready to leap out and explore. Laura scrambled after him. She saw clearly now that they were in a deep gully which was thickly treed in places. There was higher ground on either side rising to rocky outcrops and ridges. Behind and in front they were enclosed by the rugged, desolate ranges.

As she stood back while MacDougall revved the engine and endeavored to persuade the truck forward, she saw with growing dismay that it was indeed very firmly stuck, with the soft mud almost halfway up its wheels. It had evidently rained quite recently and beneath the thin dry crust the earth was wet and squelchy.

Laura called through the window to MacDougall, "It's sinking in deeper!"

He jumped down and joined her, his expression grim. "I shouldn't have chanced it," he muttered, "but it looked solid enough on top. Trouble is the surface has dried out but it's still mud underneath."

Laura knew he was angry with himself for making a bad judgment. Instinctively, she touched his arm. "You weren't to know—"

He jerked her hand away and bent to peer at the front wheels of the truck, and she stepped back, hurt by his rough dismissal, although it was only what she should have expected.

"I'll give it another go," he said, and got back in. As he did so, the truck seemed to Laura to subside even farther. She held her breath and crossed her fingers as he tried once more to extricate the vehicle from the grip of the mud.

He shouted to her, "Is it moving?"

She shook her head. "No, you're only going deeper, I think."

She heard him swear loudly, possibly thinking she was too far away to hear, but his voice carried. Laura winced, not because of the oath, but because of the self-condemnatory tone of his voice, and because she now realized that the situation was really serious.

She went up to the window. "Let me try," she said. "I'm lighter than you. Without your weight, it just might—"

"Don't be bloody silly!" he cut in roughly.

"I can drive," she insisted. "A truck's not much different from a car." It riled her that he automatically assumed she would be unable to cope.

She was determined and, in a reflex action ran around to the back of the truck for safety, only to realize that this was a mistake. The mud was softest there where the vehicle had already churned it up. She sank almost to her knees in it before she realized her folly and found herself confronted by

MacDougall, who had got out to examine the rear wheels. As she dragged her legs through the mire, he stood up and regarded her with derision. He did, however, extend a hand to pull her out.

Laura glanced down at her mud-covered feet. Her sandals were ruined, and the bottoms of her slacks were mud-caked.

MacDougall snapped, "Don't you ever think first?"

Laura could find no words to retort.

"Well, it serves you right if you've ruined those idiotic shoes," MacDougall said scathingly. "You didn't have to come. It'll do you good to find out what real discomfort is." He sounded as though he would relish her suffering. She gritted her teeth and determined not to give him that satisfaction. She would show him she was more durable than he imagined.

"No, but I'm here," she rejoined spiritedly, "so you might as well let me try to get the truck out. I couldn't make it any worse, could I?"

He regarded her with stubborn resistance. "I don't know," he drawled sarcastically. "You seem to have a propensity for doing the unexpected with somewhat disastrous results."

Laura faced him with her chin up challengingly, a determined glint in her eyes. "We're in a bit of a spot, aren't we?" she said. She knew he was worried, and hoped that it was this making him even harsher with her than he had been previously.

He considered her briefly, then said, "Okay, have a go." Evidently he didn't expect her to be able to do what he could not, but as she had said, there was little to lose. He strode back to the front of the truck and showed her how to manipulate the gears.

Laura clambered in. She suddenly felt rather nervous and wished she had not been so cocky. MacDougall gave her a few tips on how to try to get the wheels to grip but Laura knew he didn't expect results. She did exactly as he instructed, and at the same time he put all his strength behind the cab, pushing hard. The engine revved and roared until it seemed it might blow up, but the truck would not budge.

Laura clenched her teeth. She concentrated all her will-power on moving the truck forward, but there was no response, until suddenly, as she was about to give up, she felt something moving beneath her. The truck was going forward . . . yes, it definitely was . . . the wheels had got a grip at last. Elation burst through her.

"Hold tight, she's moving!" MacDougall's shout reached her through the window and gave her extra strength.

Holding her breath, Laura gripped the steering wheel, which threatened to spin away from her at every moment, and prayed she was doing the right thing. She did not even notice that it had started to rain until she could no longer see clearly through the fine drizzle on the windshield.

But her exultation was premature. A moment later she felt her control slipping. The truck was no longer inching forward, but was slowly sliding backward. Laura kept her foot down and gripped the wheel tightly, but she could not hold it. She heard MacDougall shout, "Look out!" and suddenly the steering wheel was slack, and she could feel the wheels gently subsiding into the mud once more. She put her head on her arms, bitterly disappointed.

"Hey, there's enough waterworks out here," said Mac-Dougall appearing at the cabin window.

"I wasn't crying," she retorted hotly, jerking upright. "I was just mad at myself for getting so near. . . ."

He regarded her stonily. No doubt he blamed her incompetence. Anyone but a spoiled pommie brat would have managed it, she thought bitterly. She felt all tied up in knots inside. She had so coveted his praise, his having to change his mind about her. She had so wanted his approbation, and she had paid the penalty of pride—failure.

"Well, what do we do now?" she said glumly, then realizing it was raining: "You're getting wet."

"It can't be helped. You'll have to get wet, too, I'm afraid. I don't like the look of the weather. There's a lot of thunder brewing in the distance. If we don't get the truck out onto higher ground for the night and there's a flash flood, we've had it. We're right in the creek bed here, and the whole box of tricks could be washed away."

She could tell from his voice just how seriously he regarded their predicament. Their efforts with the truck, she now realized, had taken longer than it seemed. It was already beginning to get dark, and the overcast sky was hastening it.

"What do you want me to do?" she asked.

He gave her a steady look, then said, "I'm going to try to shove some branches under the front wheels. That might do the trick. A four-wheel drive can usually handle most conditions but this is a particularly bad patch. If it doesn't work I'll have to radio Margaret Springs and get Joe to come and haul us out in the morning."

"How can I help?" Laura insisted. "I know you don't think I'm much use, but there must be something I can do."

"You can start unloading the gear," MacDougall said. "That'll lighten it a bit. Stack it up over there under the trees on that high ground. I'll rig the tarp so it won't get wet."

By the time he had rigged up the temporary shelter, it was almost dark and the rain, although intermittent, persisted. Laura had begun immediately to transfer the load from the truck to the shelter. As soon as he had erected the tarpaulin, MacDougall cut a heap of long sapling branches, and then began to dig under the front wheels with the shovel.

In a very short time, Laura's legs began to feel like jelly and her arms ached, but she did not let up. She dashed back and forth to the truck as quickly as she could, determined to win MacDougall's approval, as she was sure he believed she would give in long before the task was completed.

There were two or three items she could not move, one being the portable refrigerator. When she had shifted everything else, she staggered over to MacDougall, who was still shoveling mud and endeavoring to make ramps for both wheels.

"I've shifted everything I can carry on my own," she told him breathlessly, and was gratified to see a fleeting expression of surprise cross his face. She added, "I can't manage the fridge or the fuel drum."

As he glanced at her, there was a faint glimmer of ironic amusement in his steely eyes. He joked dryly, "Goodness, Laura, I didn't think you'd let a little thing like a portable fridge beat you!"

"This is hardly the time for sarcasm!" she snapped back.

He stood up. "I think this might do. We'll have another go, anyway. But first the fridge and the drum."

As he spoke there was a flash of lightning which illuminated the bush around them in an eerie blue glow. A long roll of thunder followed almost immediately. Laura started involuntarily, and simultaneously his arm went around her shoulders comfortingly. She pulled away instantly.

"I'm not frightened of storms!" she cried, jumping back as though scalded. "I'm not a child!"

MacDougall's eyes raked her searingly as another flash of lightning split the heavens. "No," he said, "you certainly are not."

She was aware then that they were both wet. Her shirt was clinging to her skin very revealingly, her hair was plastered around her mud-spattered face. Instinctively she folded her arms protectively across her breasts and then realized that MacDougall was laughing at her. She could put her cardigan on, of course, but as that was the only piece of dry clothing she had, there was no point in soaking that too.

"Shall we finish emptying the truck?" she reminded him.

Together they hauled the remaining items up the rather steep slope to the higher ground. It was pouring now but they disregarded the rain and ran back to the truck. Laura was unsure what MacDougall would expect of her now. She soon discovered, however.

"You take the wheel," he rapped out, and at his words a warm glow rushed over her. He was willing to let her try again! She would not fail this time, she vowed. She steeled herself and mustered all her concentration for the vital maneuver that would shift the truck out of the bog.

MacDougall shouted instructions at her, and as before put his shoulder to the vehicle to aid what the engine was attempting.

Laura stared fixedly ahead, listening for his instructions. She gripped the steering wheel with all her might, even when it seemed she did not have the strength to hold it. After what seemed an age of trying to drive through a brick wall, a new sensation vibrated through her body, a sensation she automatically recognized. The wheels were not spinning or jamming anymore, they were turning around . . . slowly turning . . . turning. . . . With her breath dry in her throat, and the steady rhythm of the windshield wipers thudding in her ears in unison with her heart, she prayed, "Let me do it this time!"

Suddenly she heard the cracking and splitting of branches and twigs, and then there was a tremendous clap of thunder right overhead. Momentarily, she lost her grip on the wheel, so startling and sharp was the explosion. She thought bleakly that she would lose all the ground she had gained. It was impossible to see ahead in the darkness, and the rain pouring down the windshield was proving too heavy even for the wipers. But, to her utter relief, the truck did not slide backward.

She heard MacDougall shouting, "Hold the left . . . keep bearing left . . . more . . . more . . . that's it . . . keep going, straight ahead now . . . keep going, that's it . . . brakes, Laura, brakes!"

Laura knew he could see better than she could, so she obeyed blindly, slamming the brakes on the instant he commanded. She felt the truck shudder to a halt. Relief left her weak and drained, and when MacDougall wrenched the door open, she almost fell out of the cab into his arms. He steadied her and then threw his arms around her and hugged her triumphantly.

"You did it!" he shouted exultantly. "You little beauty, Laura! You did it!"

She looked up into his shining wet face, dazed, incredulous.

"We made it," she whispered, clinging to him, her knees almost collapsing beneath her as the tension drained away and the realization that the truck was now safe sank in properly.

His eyes were boring into hers with a penetration she was too numbed to interpret, and when he bent his head and covered her mouth with warm, gentle lips, her last thought would have been to resist him. He had kissed her that first night to show his contempt for her, and this morning as you might soothe a troubled child, but now there was a whole world of difference, and she felt fires kindling in her that had never flamed before.

It didn't even seem strange, only perfectly natural, that MacDougall's arms should encircle her and draw her hard against him with a need that was real and without defenses, without rancor, and without restraint. The rain poured down and the thunder rumbled across the lightning-rent sky, but even though they were drenched to the skin, they were oblivious of it.

"Laura . . ." His lips released her name huskily, then strayed caressingly over her eyes, her nose, her cheeks and down the slender curve of her neck, in a voyage of tender discovery, before returning to claim her mouth once more with fresh desire. Laura, caught up in the rush of her own exploding emotions, could only register a faint alarm at the uninhibited responses of her whole being to his, but there was no way she could stop herself from being carried along on the glorious tide that was engulfing them both.

Once he lifted his head and looked deeply into her eyes, and then with a stifled groan buried his head against her sodden shoulder, sliding his hands, which were warm despite the rain, under her soaked shirt, to caress the length of her spine, and move smoothly over her shoulder blades, and down to clasp her just above the slacks she wore, his strong fingers almost meeting around her slim waist. He raised his head and looked into her face again, with, for a moment, an expression of undisguised tenderness in his eyes that brought to Laura a whole new tumult of feeling. She felt a closeness with him that was not physical and it gave her a feeling of deep inner joy.

"Robert . . ." She was unaware that she had whispered that name as she laid her head against his shoulder.

And then incredulously she felt him stiffen, and raising her eyes to his once more she saw with a shock that the tenderness had faded, the gray eyes had turned flinty again and he was looking at her coldly, as though he scarcely recognized her. A shudder ran through her as his hands fell from her waist and he stepped back. She realized with a bitter pang of disappointment that it had all been an illusion . . . already he was regretting the impulse that had made him react to her as a man to a woman.

"We're both soaked to the skin," he muttered in a gruff tone, and moved abruptly away from her. "I'd better shift the truck up nearer the camp and get a fire going. You'd better change out of those wet clothes or you'll be sick and that's one more problem I can do without."

"W . . . will we be safe now?" Laura stammered, still trembling from the encounter.

"I hope so. We're well up from the creek bed up there. Even if there's a flash flood in the night, I doubt if we'll be washed away."

Laura clambered back up to the camp while MacDougall got into the truck and slowly edged it up the incline until it was on level ground near the makeshift tarpaulin tent. Laura stood in the shelter of the tarpaulin from which little rivulets of water cascaded. She shivered and wondered how Mac-Dougall would manage to light a fire with no dry wood. Caesar, who had no love of rain, had taken shelter in the tent at the first opportunity, and now whined softly and nudged her hand. Laura tickled his ear.

"Never mind, Caesar," she said, "the boss'll get you some tea soon, I expect. Just be patient."

MacDougall strode across to them. He looked Laura up and down. "I told you to change those wet clothes. You'll catch pneumonia."

"I . . . I've got nothing dry to put on," she reminded him.

"There's a spare shirt and trousers in my pack," he said abruptly. "You'll have to make do with them until yours are dry."

"No . . . I couldn't," she protested. "You're as wet as I am. No, I'm not going to wear your clothes. . . ."

"Suit yourself," he said, in the familiar dismissive way, "but don't go sick on me. We might be stranded for days."

"Oh, no!" Laura could not help her involuntary gasp.

His eyes held hers. "No need to panic. I won't take advantage of you, don't worry. You'll be perfectly safe with me. What happened a moment ago was . . . purely reaction.

91

Just put it down to elation." His mouth twisted in a sardonic way.

Elation! Laura turned away. Yes, she supposed on his part it had only been that. Elation because they had unbogged the truck and removed the danger of it being washed away. He had kissed her because at such moments—of elation, or fear, or excitement—men often express themselves in passion. Maybe it was just as well, she thought ruefully, that it had been raining so hard and they had been standing in the mud. She gazed after him as he left her. He was fully in control of himself again now. Yes, she was quite safe with him, as he had just so plainly spelled out. He had taken pains to make sure that she understood that.

With some difficulty in the dark, she found a blanket and her cardigan. She wrapped the blanket around her waist which, in view of the darkness, was an unnecessary modesty, and removed her soaked and muddy slacks and briefs. She peeled off her shirt and slipped her arms into the sleeves of her cardigan, wrapping it securely around her and tying the belt. She wrung out her shirt and trousers and spread them over some boxes, hoping they would be dry by morning. She had kicked off her sandals earlier and now examined them with dismay. She scraped some of the caked mud off them and hoped they would survive the remainder of the trip.

When she turned around, MacDougall was watching her and, to her amazement, he had managed to get a fire going. It had evidently stopped raining at last.

There was a hint of laughter in his voice as he said, "Very fetching, I'm sure!"

"You'd better change, too," Laura said briskly, "or you'll be the sick one, and that's a problem I don't want, thank you."

He raised his eyebrows, but said only, "I'm hungry. Can you find the frying pan and kettle?"

Laura knew exactly where they were, and so while he changed into dry trousers and shirt, she put the kettle on for tea and tossed some chops and onions into the frying pan. She winced as she was slicing the onions, and realized she must have ripped open the blister on her hand sometime as she was ferrying the gear to the makeshift tent. It stung painfully, and she noticed that there was quite a bit of dirt embedded in the raw flesh of the burn.

"Rain's keeping off thank goodness," remarked Mac-Dougall.

Laura looked up from tending their meal to see him, feet astride, hands on hips looking down at her. Beyond him she could see the sky, clearing between the rain clouds, and the stars coming out.

"It's nearly ready," Laura said, feeling on edge with him.

They did not speak much as they ate. There was naturally a constraint between them because of what had happened.

Finally, MacDougall remarked, "You're a cool one, Laura."

She was startled. What did he mean? Her response to him had scarcely been cool! "Cool . . . ?" she queried warily.

His eyes roved across her face speculatively. "You're taking our predicament very calmly."

"What else can I do?" She was glad he was only referring to that.

"You could have had hysterics."

She lifted her chin. "That would fit your image of me, naturally!" She added sarcastically, "Since we aren't in any danger, I decided it would be a waste of my histrionic ability." Her tone was brittle, her glance chilly, and she was pleased to see him flinch.

"I'm sorry," he said abruptly, and sounded absolutely sincere. Laura glanced at him suspiciously, but he went on soberly, "I'm afraid I misjudged you. You're a lot tougher than you look . . . and not the sort of girl . . . well, perhaps I did jump to rather hasty conclusions. It was a great effort, anyway, shifting the truck out of the bog."

Laura was quite disarmed. "You did all the work," she muttered, confused by his changing moods. She stared at the weeping red burn on her hand as though it fascinated her. It was just something to look at, and she almost welcomed the pain it was causing her as an antidote to another deeper pain.

MacDougall noticed. "Hey . . . your hand . . ." There was unexpected concern in his tone.

She quickly turned her hand over. "It's all right."

He jumped up and came around to her side of the fire. "Let me see."

Reluctantly she showed him the burn. He held her fingers gently, and a warmth like an electric current flowed through her from his.

"It's all right," she insisted, trying to pull her hand away.

"It certainly is not," he stated firmly. "You could get a nasty infection in that." He let go of her hand and strode into the tent, returning with the first-aid box. "Now, let me attend to it," he said, in a voice that brooked no argument. Laura did not resist. Anyway, he was right. The burn could become infected now that the protective skin of the blister had been torn away.

Skillfully he cleaned the raw weal with disinfectant. She winced as it smarted and brought tears into her eyes. "Sorry," he said, "but it's necessary. This'll feel better," he added, as he applied a cooling tannic-acid jelly and then bound up her hand with expert and gentle fingers. Ministering to her in this way he was a different man altogether from the harshly critical and sneering MacDougall she had grown accustomed to, and Laura suffered a conflict of emotions such as she had never in her life felt before.

"There," he said, as he finished, "that should do the trick."

There was nothing but kindness in his tone, nothing but consideration in his eyes. Laura fervently wished he would be like this all the time, but she knew she must never forget that the real MacDougall, who, despite his apology, still despised her, lurked beneath this temporarily benign manner.

It was much too wet to sleep in the open, even if there had not been a risk of further storms, but there was at least fairly dry ground under the tarpaulin, if a rather limited space, barely enough in fact for their two sleeping bags. Laura placed herself as far from MacDougall as she could, and was mildly amused when Caesar stretched out between them, providing an effective barrier, or perhaps a deterrent to temptation. MacDougall's or hers? Laura wondered. She smiled to herself. Had he ordered the dog to sleep there?

She could not sleep for a long time. Her hand still throbbed a little, and her thoughts were chaotic. She lay listening to the steady breathing from the sleeping bag next to hers, and between them Caesar's rhythmic snores. Through the opening in the tarpaulin she could see the stars, but the night was silent after the rain and the thunder had long since been reduced to a distant murmur, the lightning to occasional far-off flashes above the ranges.

Laura had no idea what time it was. When she woke suddenly, to sit up listening to a strange roaring that was not thunder, instinctively she felt afraid, without knowing why. Caesar, too, heard it and rose growling.

"Mac . . ." Laura turned and saw him already scrambling out of his sleeping bag. "What is it?" she cried fearfully.

"Water. The creek's coming down," he said tersely. "Get out of there. We'd better scarper up to the ridge, just in case. It sounds like a big one."

Laura discarded her sleeping bag swiftly and, clutching the blanket around her, stumbled after him. It was not as dark as it had been earlier because the sky was clear and the moon was riding high.

MacDougall turned and grasped her hand. "Come on, hurry. I think we'd be all right here but we'd better not chance it."

"But what about the truck . . . all the gear. . . ." Laura protested.

"It'll have to take its chances," he said grimly. "Come on!"

He dragged her through the trees up to the ridge that overhung the plateau where they were camped above the creek bed. As they reached the top, Caesar bounding ahead of them, MacDougall suddenly pulled her against him and said in a hoarse voice, "Look . . ."

Laura did not realize what it was at first. She looked down the narrow gully, entranced by the ethereal appearance of the bush in the moonlight, and then she saw it, a wall of water, plunging down the creek bed like bolting horses, tearing bushes and saplings up by the roots, depositing some of them in the lower branches of gum trees lining the creek and carrying the rest along in its headlong plunge.

She felt spray dampen her face even at this distance. She stared in appalled fascination as the monster swallowed up the gully, leaving a foaming swirling flood behind it. For a few moments she could not even wonder whether the water had also carried away the truck and the camp—she could only feel relief that they were safe.

She was aware of MacDougall's tight hold of her, and, glancing up at his face, she saw his features were contorted in some dreadful emotion.

"Oh, my God!" he whispered hoarsely, "Oh, my God!" and abruptly released her and covered his face with his hands, and his whole body trembled violently.

Laura was stunned. The flood had been terrifying, but they were safe. She did not know what to say to him. He looked like a man whose nerve has cracked.

But the next moment he seemed to recover, and turned to her. His lips moved in a grim smile as he said, "That was a big one. Must have been a lot of rain higher up. Lucky we got the truck out in time. It'd be strung up in a tree by now, bogged or not, and we'd be in real trouble, without even the radio. We're miles from anywhere right here."

Laura shivered, appreciating, perhaps for the first time, just how savage and uncompromising this vast and desolate land could be.

From the edge of the ridge they peered down to where the camp was.

"Can you see anything?" Laura asked fearfully.

"Yes. It's still there," said MacDougall with relief. He smiled at her lamely, "Coming up here was just a precaution. . . . I didn't want to chance losing you."

Laura was startled. Then he added, "The Prof would never forgive me, would he?"

Back at the camp, MacDougall suggested making a kettle of tea. Laura was only too glad to comply. She felt unable to sleep anymore that night. She said, "It's been quite a day."

MacDougall grinned at her, all trace of his sudden strange and violent emotion up on the ridge vanished. "Quite a day. You'd better try to get some sleep, though, because we've got to reload the truck and make an early start in the morning."

"Will we be able to move on?" Laura asked doubtfully. "Won't there be worse washaways after that storm?"

"Can't tell," he answered. "Depends how localized it was. We might as well press on and hope for the best." He regarded her steadily. "I'm sure you don't want to prolong the trip any more than can be helped."

She did not answer. She knew he certainly did not.

When he urged her, she climbed back into her sleeping bag to try to get some sleep. She left him still sitting near the fire, and lay watching his silhouette as he smoked his pipe and stared reflectively into the flames as they died down to glowing coals. Laura wondered what he was thinking about. She wondered, too, how she was going to endure the next few days, which she, through her own foolish impetuosity had no alternative but to spend with him. She wished she had never met him . . . wished she had never stowed away on his truck . . . and yet, she thought miserably, she wanted to be nowhere else.

Chapter Seven

Morning dawned with clear blue skies. The sun had a sticky warmth from the moment of rising. By that time Laura was helping to load the truck. MacDougall at first suggested that because of her hand she should not, but Laura had answered him promptly, "No chivalry, remember!"

"Suit yourself, then," he had replied with his usual laconic indifference.

Reloading was easier as it was no distance to carry all the gear, and it was on the flat, not uphill, as it had been yesterday, when Laura had unloaded everything.

Laura was amazed to find that most of the water in the flooded creek bed had disappeared by morning. The only evidence of the raging torrent that had surged through the night before, carrying water down from the ranges wherever a passage could be found, was the debris hanging from the trees, tossed in ugly tangles along the edges of the creek's main course. She would never have believed in such fury, she thought, with a shudder of recall, if she had not witnessed it.

MacDougall was cautiously optimistic. "If we don't get held up too often, we should catch up with the Prof today."

"I hope so," said Laura, with feeling.

He eyed her slyly. "You'll be glad to get out of this, I'm sure."

And he would be glad to get rid of her, she thought, that's what he really meant. She said, "I don't know . . . if you'd asked me whether I'd enjoy this sort of experience, I'd probably have said no a few weeks ago, but I am enjoying it." She gazed around her. "It's so . . ." As once before, she was at a loss to explain exactly how she did feel. He was watching her closely, waiting for her to finish, so she ended rather lamely, "I feel so . . . small . . . so humble out here in these vast open spaces, and experiences like that flash flood last night put life into a new perspective somehow. It shows you how weak and insignificant you are compared with nature. . . ."

She knew it sounded trite, but it did go some way toward explaining the strange new feelings that had been creeping up on her ever since they had set out. She waited for him to laugh at her, but he didn't. Even though he smiled as he remarked, "Turning into quite a little bush philosopher, aren't you?" it was not in his usual mocking way.

She laughed at herself, however. "I suppose you think I'm being rather sentimental and trite, and typical of a spoiled city girl."

His eyes held hers. "Not at all. I believe you."

They continued packing the truck in silence. Laura wished she could understand him even a little. One minute he was pleasant to her and she thought their relationship was improving; but the next, she knew, he was just as likely to revert to sarcasm and derision, and hurt her cruelly.

This unpredictability and the enigmatic nature of the big aggressive man she had so recklessly joined just so that she could see Eric again both enraged and frustrated her. Several times that morning she had to suppress an almost overpowering desire to rush up to him and beat madly at his chest with her fists, just to get it out of her system, but of course she did not. She expended as much energy and pent-up feeling as she could on washing the truck's mud-spattered windshield, brushing the dried mud off her ruined sandals and doing her fair share of the reloading.

MacDougall did not comment on her feverish activity, but often she felt uncomfortably sure that he was watching her, and if she glanced up, she would find it was so. Those flinty gray eyes would be regarding her in a lazy speculative way.

There were no stations to visit that morning, only an old prospector, who, according to MacDougall, had spent his entire life wandering through the Outback with no more possessions than he could conveniently carry in a saddle pack on his now rather ancient horse. He had also eked out a living doing odd jobs at stations and dogging—that is, shooting dingoes and claiming a bounty from the government for their scalps.

"He also writes poetry," MacDougall told her, as the truck rattled along over rough terrain. Sometimes Laura was unable even to tell they were on a road but MacDougall seemed to have no doubts that he was going in the right direction.

"Poetry!" she exclaimed.

"It's not bad either. He might let you read some if you're interested. He used to get some of it printed in magazines years ago, but they don't care for his style anymore, apparently. It whiles away the time, I suppose, and he can say what he feels about everything. He's a real bush philosopher, old Harry Bambridge."

"Has he ever found anything—worthwhile?" asked Laura, intrigued.

MacDougall shot her a sidelong look. "If by worthwhile you mean gold or some other precious metal that can be turned into money, then the answer is no. He turns up a regular trickle of alluvial from here and there which helps to buy his tucker, but I suspect old Harry doesn't really want to strike it rich—not materially. He's rich enough already in other ways."

Laura, sensing a rebuke, and fearing a return to his contemptuous attitude toward her, fell silent. As they pressed on through the hot sticky morning, they saw plenty of evidence of washaways, but whenever MacDougall suspected trouble, he stopped and got out to investigate before risking getting bogged again. This slowed them up considerably but proved sensible. They had no trouble at all.

Laura, longing for a water hole such as the one they had stopped at before, let her thoughts anticipate the meeting with Eric. He would certainly be astonished. She smiled to herself, picturing his amazement. What would he say when he learned she had stowed away on MacDougall's truck in order to see him?

It was midday when they finally arrived at the old prospector's camp, which was in a rather bleak, barren spot between two low ranges of bare hills. There were few trees around, and those that struggled to stay alive were spindly and sparsely foliaged. Even with sunglasses on and her hat pulled down to shade her face, Laura felt as though she might ignite spontaneously at any moment. The glare of the rocks and red earth was harsh and the stony ground reflected the heat like metal.

The old prospector, Harry Bambridge, came out of his shack to welcome them. Even from a distance Laura warmed toward him. With his battered sweat-stained hat, his nicotine-stained lips and ragged teeth, he was hardly a prepossessing sight, but in the wrinkled face, tanned like a piece of old leather, the bluest of blue eyes sparkled with lively intelligence and fun, and something else which Laura was later to recognize as true contentment.

He welcomed Laura with a finger-crushing handshake in spite of the arthritis which Mac Dougall had said he now suffered from, and his smile was broad.

"First time young Mac's ever brought his girl to visit," he said, looking her over with candid but friendly appraisal.

"I'm not his girl," replied Laura, feeling she ought to be the one to explain for a change. "I'm on my way to see my brother, Professor Fairchild, who is living with some aborigines."

Harry glanced at MacDougall for confirmation. MacDougall nodded.

"Hmm," muttered Harry, lighting another limp cigarette he had just rolled from the one going out in his mouth.

101

"Hmm . . . well, who knows, eh?" He ambled off to put the kettle on, leaving Laura feeling as she had before, faintly embarrassed, especially as MacDougall was looking at her with an ironic little smile playing about his lips.

While he unloaded Harry's supplies, Laura strolled over to the fire to talk to Harry. He was mixing flour and water in a blackened pan. He looked up at her with twinkling eyes.

"Just bunging on a bit of damper for lunch," he said, and shook some currants out of a packet into the dough.

"Damper?" said Laura.

"Bushman's bread," explained Harry, spreading the mixture over the bottom of the pan. "Can't beat a good damper." He placed a blackened lid on the pan and thrust it onto the fire. "She'll only be a little while." He called to MacDougall. "You bring me any fruit, Mac? I'm clean out of raisins." He grinned at Laura. "I like a bit of dried fruit."

MacDougall strolled over. "I've put the supplies inside," he said, pushing his hat off his forehead and wiping his face on a rather grubby handkerchief. "Everything you asked for, according to Mrs. Lawson, including last week's newspapers."

"Good oh," said the old man. "Just showing your young lady how to mix a damper, Mac." He grinned at Laura again. "'Course if you can find a turkey's egg to crack into it, all the better, eh, Mac?"

MacDougall said laconically, "I don't think hunting brush turkeys would be quite Laura's style."

He and Harry chatted in a desultory way while they waited for the kettle to boil and the damper to cook. Harry stirred tea into the battered kettle, and took a look at his damper. It had risen quite a lot, Laura noticed.

"We'll go in the hut," said Harry. "She's a bit cooler in there."

"Fetch our mugs, would you, Laura?" MacDougall said, and meekly Laura ran over to the truck for them.

There were a rough table and benches in the hut. Harry spread a couple of sheets of newspaper over one end of the table and slapped the pan down on it, alongside the kettle of tea. He slopped tea into their mugs, then turned the damper out onto a very battered tin plate and cut it into three pieces.

"Mind, she's a bit hot still," he said, handing a piece to Laura.

Laura accepted the offering and caught an amused glance from MacDougall. He was expecting her to find some excuse not to eat it, she thought, and it did look rather unappetizing, like a large leathery pancake. But she was not going to offend Harry or give MacDougall any reason to crow over her.

She took a hearty bite from the corner, and to her surprise there was no need to pretend. It was delicious. And why not, she thought suddenly. It was only flour and water and currants, baked on an open fire until it was crisp and brown around the edges.

It did not seem to have occurred to Harry that she was unused to such simple fare and he seemed surprised when she complimented him on it, but his eyes sparkled with pleasure nonetheless.

After they had eaten, MacDougall said he wanted to check a couple of things on the truck, so he left Laura to talk to Harry. She was glad of the opportunity. After they had talked about his life in the bush and prospecting, Laura asked him about his poetry.

"Mac tells me you're a poet. I'd like to read some of your poems if I may."

His blue eyes gleamed suspiciously as he sucked on a cigarette. "It ain't much. Just my scribble."

"Mac said you'd had some of it published."

"Mmm. That was years ago." He grinned toothily. "You really want to read the stuff?"

"Yes, please. I'd like to very much," Laura said.

He still eyed her suspiciously, wondering perhaps if she was mocking him, as many city people might have done. However, he seemed to decide that she was sincere. "I'll get 'em for you," he said. "A few anyway. You won't have time to read 'em all now." He regarded her speculatively. "Mac's a good bloke. You won't do better'n him. One of the best. But he's not been the same since—"

He broke off as MacDougall's large frame filled the doorway of the one-room shack. MacDougall said, "Just been looking at your horse, Harry. He's a bit lame."

Harry nodded. "I was going to ask you to have a look at 'im for me, Mac. I think he's got a stone in his front left hoof, but I can't get to it." He blinked apologetically. "My eyes aren't what they used to be, nor my fingers." He spread his arthritic hands helplessly.

"I'll take a look," said MacDougall, and Laura caught a glimpse of compassion overlaid with anxiety that crossed his face as he looked at the old man.

Harry then rummaged in a box under his camp bed at the far end of the hut and thrust some tattered exercise books into Laura's hands, a little self-consciously. He ambled out and left her alone to read his work.

Laura opened the first book and read the faded ink with some difficulty, but the more she read, the more she wanted to go on. Whether it was good poetry or not, in the technical sense, she could not judge, but she did know that she was utterly captivated by the honest down-to-earth style of it, the vivid imagery of the lines of spidery handwriting. Suddenly it seemed the whole world took on a new clarity, and she felt as though she was learning all over again. It was a strange experience.

Too soon, MacDougall was back to say he had attended successfully to the horse and that it was time to move on again. Laura handed the exercise books back to Harry and told him how much she had enjoyed the poems, but she had no words to describe the depth of feeling his poetry had engendered. He accepted her compliments gracefully, but looked dubious, as though fearing she was patronizing him.

"I really do mean it," she assured him earnestly. "You say all the things I've begun to feel about this country, but I could never say them as you do. I've learned something very important today, Harry."

He clasped her hand and seemed to understand, although her words were clumsy. "Mac's a damn fool if he lets a girl like you slip through his fingers," he murmured as they went outside.

MacDougall was beckoning impatiently to Laura from the truck.

"You're right for him, lass," said Harry, fixing her with his clear blue eyes. "You'd fit in."

Laura smiled sadly. "Not with MacDougall, Harry. He despises me. I'm just a brash, superficial city slicker in his view. Anyway, he doesn't care for women at all."

"Rubbish," said Harry forcefully. "There's no red-blooded man that doesn't care for women! He just has a lot to learn. Run along, don't keep him waiting."

Laura bade the old man good-bye. She ran to the truck and squeezed into her usual position between MacDougall and Caesar.

"Sorry," she muttered, "but I didn't want to offend Harry. I did enjoy his poetry . . . it's marvelous . . . so . . . so full of life, I suppose." She added, "You've read some of it, too?"

"Yep," said MacDougall, but made no further comment.

They waved good-bye and Laura looked back as they turned with a queer kind of sadness in her heart to see the old man standing by his shack, so solitary. Then, remembering his poetry, she knew that he would scorn her pity. He was not lonely. He had become a part of the landscape. He belonged to the earth, and the sky and the trees; the birds and the animals spoke to him as clearly as any human being could.

"He must be quite old," Laura remarked.

"Too old to live there much longer," said MacDougall, and there was a hint of sadness in his voice that surprised Laura. "One day soon I'm either going to have to take him back to town because he can't look after himself anymore or I'll come by and find he's pegged out."

"Wouldn't it be better if he lived nearer civilization?" Laura asked. "He ought to be in a home at his age."

MacDougall drew his lips together. "It would kill him if he was forced to go into an old folks' home or a geriatric hospital." The slight catch in his gravelly voice touched Laura deeply. MacDougall cared about the old man far more than she would ever have imagined. Suddenly MacDougall had a new dimension for her.

She said, "He'd rather die out here."

"Yes. But it might not happen quickly and mercifully. He might be taken desperately ill, with no one to help him. That's what bothers me."

"Does he have a radio?"

"No. Won't hear of it. Says he doesn't know how to work one and won't learn. He's a cussed old devil, very independent. Anyway, it'd take a couple of days to get to him even if he called for help. He flatly refuses to live somewhere more accessible. He loves these ranges. I've tried to persuade him to at least come a bit nearer to civilization but he won't."

"Don't . . ." said Laura suddenly.

MacDougall looked at her sharply. "I thought you just said he ought to be in a home. It would be for his own good after all."

"There are more important things," said Laura slowly, "than one's own good, in that sense. He knows better than we do what is for his own good. Leave him alone, Mac. Whatever happens to him, I think he would rather that than anything do-gooders might force on him."

A faint smile crossed his lips as he negotiated a rugged dip in the road across a dried-up creek bed. He glanced quickly at Laura and said, "You surprise me, Laura. I thought you'd think me cruel and callous if I said that's what I intended to do. There's more to you, obviously, than meets the eye."

There was nothing she could say to that, and since he did not pursue the subject, she contented herself with quiet reflection on the unusual morning, old Harry Bambridge and his extraordinarily moving poetry. It was strange, but since this morning even the scenery seemed to her clearer, more well defined and her senses sharper.

It was midafternoon and she had dozed briefly, to waken abruptly as they jolted to a halt. MacDougall jumped down from the truck.

"What's the matter?" she asked, fearing they had broken down or were bogged again.

"They've gone," he said shortly. "The Prof and the tribe. Left. This is where I expected to find them."

Laura jumped down, too. She looked around, bewildered. "Left?" she echoed foolishly.

MacDougall was stirring the remains of a campfire with a stick he had picked up. "Yep, but not today. Fire's quite cold. Day or two ago, I reckon."

Laura was stricken. "But where would they have gone? Aren't they expecting you with supplies?" Suddenly she had a horrible feeling she was never going to find Eric.

MacDougall looked up. "It's all right. There'll be a message, I expect." He looked around for a moment, then walked over to a tree with a hollow in it, quite low down. Laura remembered then that he had said Eric would leave a message. She watched him poke around in the hole with a stick. He turned to say with a smile, "Just in case there are any occupants!" He added, reaching in, "Ah, I thought so." He drew out an old tobacco tin. As he opened it, Laura ran swiftly to his side, eager to know what the message was.

MacDougall was scanning the piece of paper he had taken from the tin as she reached him. "What does it say?" she asked, on tenterhooks.

MacDougall frowned briefly. "They've gone towards the west, back to their old tribal grounds. It seems there are sacred sites there that they've finally agreed to show him. Quite a triumph for the Prof. He's been hoping he might turn up something special. He says there are paintings . . . anyway, read it yourself." He thrust the note into Laura's hand. She scanned it eagerly, happy just to see Eric's familiar handwriting.

"Do you know where it is . . . how to get there?" she asked, anxiously.

MacDougall nodded. "Fortunately, I do. We won't make it today, though. There's some very rough country between us and them, I'm afraid. We have to travel right into the heart of the ranges. There are very few roads."

Laura tried not to let her disappointment at this setback show, or her apprehension. She shrugged and said lightly, "Oh, well, it'll be all the more exciting for the anticipation, I suppose."

MacDougall wiped his forehead. He was sweating more than usual, Laura noted absently, as he grinned at her. "I suppose you fancy yourself as sort of a female Stanley." He laughed and mimicked her voice in a shrill falsetto, "Ah, Professor Fairchild, I presume!"

Laura was not offended. She laughed, too. He imitated her rather well, even her English accent, but she did not mind. If only, she thought, there could be this friendly aspect all the time, and never those moments when there was a cutting edge to his remarks that hurt and bewildered her.

"We'd better get cracking," MacDougall said. "We might as well cover as much ground as we can before nightfall. We've been lucky so far, but we don't know what we might find crossing some of the creek beds and we'll have quite a few to cross on this trip."

They started to walk back to the truck. Suddenly an enormous lizard reared its head up in front of them. Laura froze and let out a shrill scream. MacDougall clasped her arm. "It's all right. He won't hurt you. Just an old man parentie."

With a baleful look, the large yellow spotted lizard, which was all of a meter in length, galloped toward the nearest tree and vanished up it with Caesar in hot pursuit. MacDougall looked at Laura's white face and laughed. "I only hope we don't meet any dinosaurs!"

"I've never seen one so huge," she said in a small voice. "It was like a dragon!"

"I'm afraid I don't see myself as St. George," he replied dryly.

Laura let that remark pass without comment. MacDougall offered her a can of beer but she declined and had a mug of water from the canvas water bag that hung from the tailboard. It was still very hot, although less humid now. For the remainder of daylight they pressed on, through seemingly trackless terrain, although, as always, MacDougall seemed to know where he was going even when paths petered out and, to Laura's eyes, disappeared altogether.

Just before sunset, they entered a valley ringed by rugged red cliffs bare of all vegetation on their rocky slopes. There was a narrow stream running along the floor of the valley, and apart from the flooded creek where they had camped last night this was the only creek with water in it Laura had seen during the entire journey.

"We'll camp here," said MacDougall, urging the truck onto rising ground under a clump of gums that seemed to grow right out of the rocks. Laura was relieved to escape from the stifling heat in the truck to the cool shade of the trees. They both flung themselves down on the still-warm rocks for a few minutes' rest. MacDougall looked weary, Laura thought in surprise.

She watched the last rays of the sun slant across the valley, turning the sheer rocky cliffs into a succession of fiery colors, from red, to orange, to gold and finally to a deep shadowy purple.

"I wish I could paint," she said at last. "The colors are so vibrant, so unreal, and they are changing all the time. It's fantastic."

MacDougall said nothing. Presently he got up and went about the routine business of making the fire. The sun's heat had gone and immediately there was a welcome coolness in the air. Laura suggested she would make a damper for their tea.

MacDougall laughed. "All right, go ahead!"

MacDougall had a saucepan as well as a frying pan, she had discovered, so while a can of braised steak, to which she had added some extra chopped onion and tomato, was heating on the coals, Laura mixed the dough for a damper, using mixed fruit from a packet she had found in MacDougall's pack. To her delight it worked very well and presently earned her a compliment from her enigmatic companion on the other side of the fire.

Later, they watched the moon rise. It was a full moon and it rose huge and blood-red over the distant range beyond the end of the valley. It seemed so close that for a moment Laura fancied it balanced on the ridge trying to make up its mind whether to take off into the sky or roll down into the valley. Its fieriness reflected the savage red heart of the country, she thought, and the savage red heart of MacDougall.

"Savage moon . . ." she murmured in a low voice.

"What's that?" MacDougall, a few feet away, was quietly puffing on his pipe, Caesar stretched out contentedly near his feet.

Laura hadn't realized she had spoken aloud. "One of Harry's poems," she said, "a rather evocative one, I thought. The moon was blood-red the other night, too."

"It's the dust haze," MacDougall said prosaically, and then, "I don't remember that poem."

Laura did. Slowly she recited it. It was quite short and had so impressed her she remembered every word after only two swift readings. It described the relentless, unforgiving savagery of the land, and yet, like the moon which often rose blood-red and angry, but later turned to a gentler gold, the land, too, Harry had written, could be gentle and protective and welcoming.

". . . and the land, like a woman, is true. Who loves her deeply, she loves him, too," Laura finished.

"You have a remarkable memory," MacDougall observed.

She glanced at him, feeling slightly foolish, thinking he probably thought her and the poem sentimental. "I liked it," she defended. "It sort of . . . says what I feel. . . ."

He chuckled. "Bush getting under your skin, is it?"

"I suppose so." She knew he was laughing at her and wished she had kept her thoughts to herself.

"Just a phase," he said dismissively. "People come out here and rave about the wide-open spaces, the fabulous colors, the freedom from the rat race and how lucky people are who can live away from the cities, but they don't really mean it. They're only too glad to get back to their cozy little pigeonholes. Leave them here for a week and it begins to get on their nerves, the emptiness drives them mad." His eyes were suddenly cold and censorious again. "Oh, yes, it's very romantic. See the real Australia, all the travel brochures say—and they come in droves to do just that, but the novelty would soon wear off if they had to stay. . . ."

He sounded personally bitter, which perplexed Laura. His contempt was not just directed at her, she felt sure, although he was doubtless reminding her that she had been in the

Outback a mere few days. She wondered again about his strange way of life, operating what must be a far from lucrative contracting business while preferring to let a manager run his cattle station. It still didn't make sense, but she doubted if anything about this odd man ever would, to her. She longed to ask him about himself, but in all their time together so far he had divulged no information about himself, and any questions she had dared to ask that verged on being personal he had sidestepped. She could see that he was in no mood now for probing.

She said, "I might stay . . . because I want to."

"Stay?" His eyebrows rose.

"I want to help Eric," she said, with a spurt of determination in her voice. "I'm sure he could do with an assistant, and I'd like to do something worthwhile—"

His contemptuous laughter cut her short. "Oh, that is a nice romantic notion," he mocked. "But if I were you, I'd forget it. The Prof won't want you as a millstone around his neck, and nor will the tribe." His tone was scathing. He looked her up and down. "You don't really have any idea how the Prof lives, do you? You wouldn't last a week."

She felt her anger rising and wished she had not been foolish enough to speak, to imagine he would applaud her idea.

"I'll let Eric be the judge of that," she retorted haughtily. "I don't think you know me very well."

"I know that girls like you are often full of romantic ideas that seldom last long. You're not cut out for Outback life, and certainly not for wandering around with a tribe of aborigines. In any case, I'm quite sure the Prof wouldn't hear of it."

Laura remained silent. She knew she could not change his opinion of her. Besides, it was Eric she needed to convince. She hugged her knees and watched the moon turn gold as it climbed beyond the haze, turning from savage to benign. Like MacDougall, she thought. Savage to benign, then back again, so you never knew where you were with him.

She stole a sidelong look at him. His profile was as rugged as the hills, as uncompromising and as mysterious. To her he was cruel and mocking, but to others he was a 'good bloke,'

111

as Harry Bambridge had said, and as his affectionate concern for the old man proved. Mrs. Gordon had said so, too, and even Mrs. Burdekin back in Camel Creek. They all admired and respected MacDougall, but Laura doubted if any of them knew him any better than she did. She had been with him constantly for three days and nights. In those circumstances you would normally get to know a person quite well, she reflected, but not MacDougall. He was as much an enigma as ever.

She sighed and thought of Camel Creek, wondering vaguely in which direction it lay. It might as well be on the moon itself, she mused, it seemed so far away at this minute. And London, England, might as well be in another universe.

"More tea?" she said suddenly, using the mundane to break the charged atmosphere that had sprung up between them.

"Thanks," he said, and handed her his mug.

She sprang up and went over to the fire to refill both their mugs from the kettle. She handed his to him, as careful as he was not to let her fingers touch his. They were both wary of physical contact since last night's regretted moment of passion. Laura found it most difficult in the truck, where the constant jolting brought them together so often. Once at least today she had woken from a doze to find her head leaning against his shoulder.

As he took the mug from her, he said, "How's the hand?"

"It's all right," she answered.

"You'd better let me dress it again."

"No! I mean, it's all right . . . I can manage," she protested. She did not think she could bear his care and attention, which almost amounted to tenderness and yet was nothing of the kind, at least not of the kind she wanted from him.

Presently they dragged out their sleeping bags and settled down for the night, using a big flat rock as a base, with a suitable distance between them and Caesar on guard as usual. Laura was awakened some hours later by the dog whimpering. She sat bolt upright with a start.

"Caesar," she whispered coaxingly, not able to see him at first. "Here, boy, what's up?"

112

The dog bounded across to her and then back to where MacDougall lay, but Laura had already heard the groans and was swiftly scrambling out of her sleeping bag. She dashed across to him. He was lying on the rock, but had rolled almost onto the rough ground around it. He had thrown off his sleeping bag and it lay some distance away, as did his blanket, both tossed aside as though in a fury.

For a moment Laura looked down at his moaning form, nonplussed. First she decided he must be having a nightmare, so she knelt and grasped his shoulder, shaking him, and thinking how ironic it was that she should now wake *him* from a nightmare. He did not respond, however, but began thrashing his arms about, shouting, "The water . . . the water . . . oh, God, the water!"

Laura laid her hand on his forehead. It was hot and covered with beads of perspiration. He was quite obviously delirious with fever. A chill, she thought, and ran to rescue his sleeping bag. The first thing to do was to get him back into it. This was no easy task, but she managed it, and he seemed quite unaware of what was happening. He just kept muttering and mumbling unintelligibly while Laura became more and more worried. This was no ordinary chill. And then it dawned on her.

"Of course, it's malaria!" she gasped aloud. Her father had suffered from the disease, so had her brother. She remembered her father's recurring bouts from when she was a small child. Her mother had always dismissed them as colds or flu, but the hot and cold sweats had been more than that, and he had always been delirious.

She looked down at MacDougall, wondering what to do. If he was subject to bouts, she thought, he probably carried medication, so there was bound to be something in the first-aid box. She fetched it out of the truck. There were bandages, ointments, a tourniquet and various bottles of tablets and pills. Quinine was somewhat out of date, she knew, so possibly it would be some other drug she was looking for. Rapidly she eliminated everything that was readily recognizable like aspirin, antibiotics and indigestion tablets, as well as other common medications, which left two products she did not recognize. Neither gave a clue as to what they were treatment for, but both were prescriptions. Laura glanced at MacDougall, quite temporarily, and wondered if he could tell her which was the right drug. She tried to rouse him but there was no response.

Laura sat back on her heels. What if he should die, she suddenly thought with a wave of panic, but it was not the terrible prospect of being all alone that frightened her, simply that she couldn't bear it if he died.

"Don't die," she whispered softly, "please don't die, Mac . . . I . . . I love you!"

It was the first time she had admitted it. But how could she love him? She had known him a scant few days. She had quarreled and bickered with him constantly. He despised her and treated her as a spoiled child. He would never see her as anything else, despite his apology for misjudging her and his reluctant admiration when she drove the truck out of the bog. He had only seemed to unbend in those moments of unguarded passion, and had very bluntly warned her off afterward.

She looked down at his dear face and wiped the moisture from his forehead once more. He tried to push his way out of the sleeping bag again, but she tucked his arm back inside and zipped it up. Suddenly, he opened his eyes and looked hard at her, his gaze glassy and feverish in the pale moonlight.

"Mac . . ." Laura whispered. "You've got a fever . . . malaria . . . isn't it?" She waited for some response but none came. She held up the bottle she thought the most likely. "Is this what you take for it? Or is it this?" She showed him the other one.

He continued to stare unseeingly, and she was afraid he was going to lapse into semiconsciousness again, but suddenly he wrested his arm out of the sleeping bag again and grabbed hers.

"Don't leave me . . . don't go . . . please . . . I love you so much. There's no need for us to quarrel . . . I'll do anything you want . . . only don't go. . . ."

Laura felt as though the moon had fallen out of the sky onto her. "Mac . . . you're delirious," she murmured. "You don't know what you're saying. . . ." She was thunderstruck, but her heart was racing and a feeling of exultation was racing through her like wildfire.

He slumped back, eyes closed, still grasping her wrist tightly. Laura just looked at him incredulously. Could it be . . . could what had happened to her, in spite of everything, have been happening to him too? She hardly dared believe it, but it was possible that all this time he had been fighting it, not wanting her to realize, perhaps believing that she . . . Of course, it would account for . . . almost everything. . . . A surge of tenderness washed over her as her wild erratic thoughts piled up on top of one another.

"Oh, Robert . . ." she whispered at last. "Oh, *Robert* . . . my darling!" The name she had longed to but never dared use slipped out unwittingly in the intimacy of the moment.

"Are you still there?" he mumbled. "Say you love me . . . say you forgive me . . . say we'll start again . . . just say it, my darling. . . ."

"I love you," Laura whispered. "I know it's crazy, but I really do love you, and of course I forgive you, and of course we can start again. Oh, Robert, my darling, I love you so much!"

He opened his eyes and smiled without looking at her. "I know you do really," he whispered through dry lips. "I know you hate being here . . . you don't belong . . . but I thought it was me you hated. . . ."

"I thought you hated me," Laura whispered.

He suddenly seemed to focus on her face, and then his eyes closed and he muttered, "Hate you? Don't be so absurd. You drive me mad, you witch. I can't sleep for wanting you. I want to hold you in my arms every minute of the day and night . . . you're driving me crazy. . . ."

"I'm sorry. . . ." Laura said softly, smiling to herself. Then, mindful of his condition, she tried again, as he seemed more rational: "Tell me, Robert, are these your malaria tablets? I must know. . . ."

He looked at the bottle she held out. "Tablets . . . yes, tablets . . . must have the tablets." He clasped the bottle tightly in his hand, nodding his head. Laura pried his fingers from the bottle, and he caught at her hand, holding it in a viselike grip. "Don't leave me . . . we'll go away together . . . anywhere you want. . . ." He slumped back, muttering incoherently.

"I'm just going to get some water," Laura said soothingly. She would have to trust that he had been aware enough to recognize the bottle as the right one, she decided. "I won't be a minute."

She tore her head away and ran to the water bag with a mug to fill. As she did so, MacDougall cried out in an anguished voice, "Valerie! Valerie! Darling . . . come back! Come back!"

His cries echoed through the stillness of the night. Laura stopped in her tracks and looked around. Suddenly it seemed as though the world spun out from under her feet, leaving her suspended in a black and limitless universe. Agonizingly, she heard him whimper, "Valerie . . . don't leave me. . . ."

Chapter Eight

Laura sat close beside MacDougall for the rest of the night, wiping his brow intermittently with a handkerchief wrung out in cold water. From time to time she rose and paced back and forth just to stretch her stiffened limbs. Her thoughts and emotions were in turmoil, and uppermost was a burning curiosity about, and jealousy of, someone called Valerie. A woman that MacDougall loved.

She remembered that Mrs. Gordon had said he had been married. Was Valerie his wife? Perhaps she had left him. Laura tried to imagine what kind of woman MacDougall would love, and a procession of faces haunted her until the gray dawn crept stealthily over the bush. She found to her shame that she hated the woman called Valerie, not because MacDougall loved her and she stood between her, Laura, and him, because that was not even true—MacDougall would never have wanted her even if there had been no one else—but because, whoever she was, he was lost without her, unhappy, lonely and embittered.

By morning MacDougall's fever had abated. He slept

quietly, breathing steadily, no longer tossing about or mumbling in delirium. His brow was dry, Laura saw thankfully. At daylight she moved away from him and lit the fire. The kettle was boiling and she was spooning tea into it when he called.

"Laura . . ."

"Mac . . ." She ran to him, knelt near him. "How are you feeling?" She peered into his face anxiously.

"Ghastly." His eyes raked her face as though trying to remember something. "Laura . . . I think I had a touch of fever." He brushed his hand wearily across his forehead and through his tousled hair.

"You certainly did! You gave me a terrible fright, thrashing about and groaning. I didn't know what was the matter with you at first. Then I guessed it was malaria. My father and brother both had it and I remembered when they'd had bouts at home. I guessed you'd have some medication."

"You found it and gave it to me?" he murmured, surprised.

"Well, you wouldn't expect me to let you rave on and catch pneumonia without doing something, would you?" Laura returned smartly. She added honestly, "Actually I didn't do much. I just heaved you back into your sleeping bag after you'd thrown it off. . . ."

"You got me back into it?"

She shot him a reproachful look. "Of course. You fought a bit but I managed it in the end. I didn't think you should lie in the open all night with just two thin blankets over you, the state you were in, even if I could have kept them on you." She paused, a little disconcerted by the scrutiny he was giving her, then added, "As for your medication, it was a choice of two bottles and despite your delirium you seemed to know which one was the right one."

He ran agitated fingers through his hair. "You're a good kid."

Laura swallowed hard. He would only ever think of her as a child, whatever she did.

"I hope my ramblings weren't too blasphemous or obscene," he said, somewhat sheepishly.

Laura was tempted to ask him who Valerie was, but she

could not muster the courage. Without looking directly at him, she said, "No . . . it was mostly incomprehensible."

He seemed relieved. Obviously he had no recollection of her being with him last night and had no idea he had believed she was Valerie. Laura was paradoxically glad. It meant that he would not remember what she had said, either. He must not guess her feelings, especially now. He would mock her cruelly, she felt sure, and brutally remind her that he had already warned her against such foolishness. She knew she could not bear the humiliation.

"I'm terribly thirsty," he said, as he began to unzip his sleeping bag.

"Stay there," Laura urged. "I've made tea but I'll get you a drink of water first."

MacDougall seemed relieved not to have to make the effort to get up yet. Laura guessed he must be feeling very weak.

"Haven't had a bout for a couple of years," he told her, when she handed him the mug of water. "Thought I was clear of it at last. Must have been getting wet the other night." He grinned at her apologetically. "Sorry, if I scared you. I'm not surprised you panicked. You might have been stranded out here all alone if I croaked."

"I didn't panic," Laura retorted huffily. "And I didn't think you were very likely to die." She was afraid she might give herself away so she added quickly, "Where did you pick it up? Not in Australia?"

He was eyeing her speculatively and she found his gray-eyed gaze very disconcerting. It was as though he was again trying to remember something. He said, "No, it was in South America. I was on a trip a few years back and we were stranded in a small village after losing all our gear and medical supplies in an accident on the river. Actually it isn't malaria, but something very similar. It has an exotic name which I've quite forgotten. I was told that, with modern drugs, recurrence is rare, but I keep something by me just in case. Just as well I do."

Laura nodded. "I'll get breakfast." She was glad to escape. MacDougall joined her a few minutes later. He looked drawn and exhausted and walked unsteadily. His face was grayish. He ate the food she had prepared and drank two mugs of scalding tea. His eyes still had a glazed look as though the fever had not completely left him yet.

"I could do with a shower right now," he said, "and I bet you could too. It was pretty hot yesterday."

"I managed to have a bit of a wash in the creek," Laura said, "but there's only a trickle and it's rather muddy."

"You'll be able to indulge yourself in a good wallow when we reach the tribal grounds," MacDougall promised. "There's a good water hole there, better than the last one we stopped at." He surveyed her whimsically. "For someone who is used to being straight out of a beauty salon, you're bearing up very well." There was scarcely a hint of the mocking MacDougall behind the veiled compliment, but Laura knew that whatever happened he would always view her profession, and her, as superficial and frivolous.

"Are you sure you're well enough to drive today?" Laura asked anxiously. "You look awfully gray. Shouldn't we rest up here for a bit longer?"

He smiled wryly. "Magnanimous of you, Laura, but I'm not going to keep you from your brother any longer than I can help."

She said, "Will the return journey to Camel Creek be quicker than coming out?"

He nodded. "We've got a couple of stops, that's all, mainly mail and papers for a couple of outlying stations." He gave her a teasing look. "But I thought you'd made up your mind to stay and help the Prof with his work?"

The remark needled her, but she refused to be goaded. "I'm not so stupid I don't realize I couldn't do that right away," she retorted, with only mild asperity. "I haven't got any clothes for one thing. I'd have to go back for my things. . . ." She trailed away, realizing that the only way she could return would be with Mac on his next trip, and as he was dying to get rid of her now, he would hardly take kindly to having her along again. Perhaps he would suggest some alternative arrangement. He did not, however, make any comment at that moment.

He said, "Living the way Eric does will be tougher than roughing it along with me. You haven't the faintest idea what you'd be letting yourself in for."

Laura firmed her mouth defensively, but did not answer. She could have told him that she felt able to bear any physical hardship now. It was only the emotional upheaval he had caused in her that was unbearable. She had never expected to fall in love with a man like him.

"I could drive for a bit this morning," she ventured at last. "That would give you a chance to rest. . . ."

He was adamant. "That won't be necessary. I'm all right now."

As she began to bridle, he added, "Not that I don't think you're capable. In fact you've convinced me you're astonishingly competent at many things."

"Oh, thanks," she replied, with bitter irony.

"Laura . . ."

She looked up sharply at his inquiring tone.

"Laura, what's the matter?"

"Nothing . . ."

He did not accept her denial. "You're just about at the end of your tether, aren't you? I admit it has been pretty grueling. . . ."

"But you warned me!" she responded snappishly. "You told me the risks. Moral—don't take a woman with you. Like on ships. They bring bad luck. Isn't that the story?"

He agreed. "Women were once supposed to bring bad luck to ships, yes, but I'm not blaming you for our little difficulties. In fact you've been very useful in getting us out of them. Besides, I didn't bring you, you came in spite of me!"

He smiled cheeringly, but Laura was in no mood to be jollied along. She felt tense, and brittle, as though she might shatter into a thousand pieces at any moment.

"There's no need to rub it in," she answered churlishly. "I know perfectly well I've only got myself to blame for any discomfort and inconvenience, but I'm not complaining, am I?"

"No, but you're behaving rather oddly this morning. You're as edgy as a dingo on a leash."

121

"I didn't get much sleep last night," she pointed out.

"No, I guess you didn't. My fault, and I'm sorry. I'm very grateful to you, Laura . . . really. . . ." He reached out and touched her briefly, which made sudden tears rush into her eyes. She couldn't bear it when he was kind.

She said shakily, "More tea?"

Instantly he laughed. "Laura! Why do you always say, 'More tea?' like someone in a play, when you want to change the subject?"

"Do I?" She was disconcerted.

"Yes, you do." He studied her closely for a moment. "I think I know what's the matter with you."

"You do?" She was aghast. Did he remember what she had said to him last night after all?

He nodded, and held out his mug for more tea, still looking at her. She trembled as she poured the tea into his and then her own mug, wishing the earth would open up and swallow her.

At last he said slowly, "You're suddenly scared of meeting up with Eric, aren't you?"

Laura stared at him, half in relief, half in surprise.

He went on, "You're afraid deep down that he is going to be angry with you, for tracking him down like this, and you're terrified he won't be pleased to see you. You know in your heart of hearts, Laura, I'm sure, that what you propose is impossible, but you're doggedly sticking to it regardless."

Laura was so relieved that he was unaware of her foolish misunderstanding of his delirium ravings, and therefore her true feelings about him, that she could not answer for a moment. Finally, she conceded, "Well, maybe I am a bit anxious about seeing Eric. It's been a long time. We haven't seen each other for years."

MacDougall toyed with his mug of tea, swirling the liquid around and around. He looked at her pityingly. "You won't find that Eric has the answers," he said. "We have to solve our own problems, you know."

Laura did not reply. She knew he was right, and that her headlong rush to find Eric was in a way pure escapism, a desire to shift the responsibility onto someone else's shoulders. She drew a deep breath. It was painful to have to acknowledge that Mac had been able to see through her so much better than she had been able to fathom him. It made her feel very vulnerable.

He stood up. "Well, we'd better get moving. The sooner we put you out of your misery, the better."

She stood up too, and he strode over to her purposefully, catching her unawares as he placed his fingers under her chin and tilted her face up so that she was forced to look fully at him. She prayed he would not see everything she was feeling revealed in her eyes.

He said encouragingly, "Don't worry . . . I'm sure the Prof *will* be glad to see you, and he'll help if he can."

She pulled her face away from him. His touch electrified her, and she was terrified he would guess why she trembled. Tears of frustration filled her eyes, and the better to hide her true feelings she hit out at him.

"Oh, don't be so—so patronizing!" she cried, and stamped her foot hard.

He stepped back as though she had dealt him a physical blow, then reached for her placatingly. "Laura . . ."

She sidestepped and faced him angrily. The tension of the long night had proved too much. Her feelings had been thrown into worse turmoil than ever by the revelation that MacDougall loved another woman, and her only defense now was anger.

"Don't touch me," she whipped out. "Leave me alone, can't you. I'm sick to death of you and your superiority. You think you're so damned perfect, don't you, and it's fun to mock me any way you can. I wish I'd never set eyes on you and your rotten truck and your stupid dog! And I don't even care if I never see my brother. I expect he's as bad as you are. You men are all the same—vain, arrogant, feelingless, just making use of others and not caring a bit how they feel. I . . . I think you're utterly despicable!"

The words poured out until she became incoherent and had to stop. As the spate of fury abated, she stared at him, appalled, at his ashen face, his fever-sunken eyes, at the tight line of his mouth, the implacable way he stood there letting her rave on, making an absolute fool of herself. As if she hadn't done that enough times already!

His silence, and the sudden stillness of the bush around them after her outburst, enveloped her like a suffocating cloak. She stood stock-still for a moment, as shocked as he was, and then, with a choking sob, wheeled around and began to run. She heard him call, "Laura . . . come back!" but it echoed in her tormented mind as it had last night—"Valerie . . .come back!" She kept on running. She had to put as great a distance between them as she could. It was the only thought in her head. She just couldn't bear to be near him any longer.

Chapter Nine

Laura ran as though impelled by some unseen force. She thought of nothing except that she must get away from MacDougall. It was foolish and irrational, but her mind was not in a prudent or rational state after the tensions of the previous night. Emotion had replaced reason, and the only thing that motivated her now was the urgent need to flee from the thing that oppressed her.

She stumbled aimlessly over rocks and fallen branches, every impediment only making her run faster and farther. It was only sheer exhaustion that finally forced her to stop. She clutched her side where a nagging stitch was making her bend almost double, and her breath came in choking sobs.

"I wish I'd never come . . . I wish I'd never come . . ." She sobbed as she leaned against a tree and wiped a grimy hand across her face, which was hot and perspiring and already streaked with red dust. Then, as she looked around, gradually the lunacy of what she had done penetrated.

She was completely hemmed in by the bush. The trees were motionless in the still morning air, the silence disturbed only by the occasional bird call, faint rustlings, the churring of insects. Above, the sky was already a hard blue bowl, cloudless, with the sun climbing hotly above the glaring red hills that ringed her. She gazed around anxiously. How far was she from the camp? Which direction had she come from? Suddenly she was not sure. It all looked the same. The bush she had begun to love was all at once threatening; the smooth white trunks of the ghost gums all looked the same and seemed to crowd in on her. There were no paths, only the rough rocky ground, the red dust and the sparse undergrowth and clumps of grasses.

Not yet admitting to her growing fear, she walked carefully around. It should be easy enough to follow her own tracks back to the camp. She couldn't have come all that far. She dragged her hand wearily across her brow again. The memory of her headlong dash was fragmented. She had no idea for how long she had plunged through the bush, even what time it had been exactly when they were having breakfast. But she couldn't have been running for more than a few minutes—she would have become exhausted quite quickly.

Still uncertainty prevailed. Anger had lent her strength, frustration had pushed her to the limit. She had run wildly, meandering all over the place to avoid obstacles. As she searched with increasing desperation for certain signs of her tracks, and found nothing conclusive, she knew finally and despairingly that she was lost.

A wave of panic assailed her. She whirled frantically around, but the trees seemed to close in on her more closely than before.

"Mac . . ." she called thinly, her voice dying in her parched throat, coming out as barely a whisper.

He would look for her, wouldn't he? She remembered some of what she had said to him and flinched. He would scarcely be pleased about that, or the fact that she had become lost.

"What a crazy thing to do!" she wailed. "What a complete idiot I am!"

She was clearheaded now. The tension had eased, the pent-up emotion was expended and she was able to see her rash action in the cold-blooded way MacDougall must be viewing it—as stupid and irresponsible. But, at the same time, she began to know real fear. She had run off unthinkingly, she had rushed helter-skelter in a dozen different directions. MacDougall might never find her. . . .

She sank onto a fallen log, her head in her hands. What on earth had possessed her to do such a mindless thing? She knew the reason, but that did not excuse the lunacy of ignoring all the rules and getting herself lost. MacDougall would have every right to be livid with her. If he found her . . .

For a few minutes she sat dejected, resigned to her fate. But despairing though she felt, her instinct for survival was nevertheless strong. Giving in was not something she did easily. As her heartbeat slowed back to normal, and her breathing became easier, the stitch disappeared and she began to look at her predicament practically.

She had to find the camp and MacDougall again, and she had to do it intelligently, not rush all over the place in a crazy panic.

"MacDougall!" She called his name loudly, but her voice sounded pitifully weak, and seemed to bounce back at her from the nearest tree. She listened but there was no answer. She bit her lip anxiously.

"If I could just see over the trees," she thought, "I might be able to spot the truck. . . ."

That thought was immensely cheering. It galvanized her into a positive action. All she had to do, she thought, was climb a tallish tree, and doubtless she would then command a view of the valley that would show her which direction she must take. It was easier said than done, however. None of the nearby trees offered any footholds close enough to the ground, or if they did, there was too great a gap before the next branches for her to bridge.

"I've got to do something," she said aloud. She called out again, but it was no use. There was no answer.

She thought ruefully of what MacDougall had said at the beginning: "If you behave yourself and don't cause any trouble, okay, but if you do I might just decide to let you find your own way back." She remembered his glowering face, forbidding in the firelight, and how she had been sure he didn't really mean it.

Not then. But now? He wouldn't go and leave her, would he? He might not be callous enough to do that, she thought tremulously, but what if he failed to find her. . . .

She tried to remember where the sun had been when it rose that morning, behind the camp or in front of it. She thought it had been behind, but suddenly she could not be sure even of that. Her mind had been in too much turmoil since last night to notice such unimportant things. Nevertheless, she strained, trying to recall.

If the sun was behind me as I packed the gear in the truck, she thought, then the camp must be that way. . . . She faced in the direction which that reasoning indicated, but still felt unsure. Hadn't it glared in her eyes as she stowed her sleeping bag away? She faced the other way, but was no more certain. There were places where the undergrowth looked trampled, the dust churned up, but her footprints seemed to be all over the place and she could find no definite trail of them.

She sighed with frustration. Then she had another idea. She would climb the nearest hill. It would take her farther away perhaps but at least she ought to be able to see where she was sooner or later. She set out toward the nearest rocky hillside. It proved farther than she had expected. She crossed a dry creek bed, picked her way over and around rough stones, and through prickly bushes, her already tattered sandals affording poor protection against the spines and burrs and the small stones that flicked up under her toes.

At last she began to scramble upward, over boulders and between heaps of rocks tumbled there in some dim archaeological past. The only heartening part was that surely she would not have to go far before she would spot the truck, or perhaps even MacDougall. She glanced at her watch. She must have been lost well over an hour already. He would be livid all right.

She reached a level spot and turned to look back, shading her eyes against the sun's glare. Spread out before her was the whole valley, with glimpses of the creek meandering through the swards of bush. For a moment she quite forgot she was lost, the view was so magnificent, and when pied butcher-birds began a melodious duet far below her, she caught her breath, thrilling to the sound.

A moment later, there was another sound which at first she thought was still the birds. Then she realized it had a human quality.

"Cooooo . . . ee!"

The long note followed by the short sharp *ee* carried over the bush piercingly, and she knew it could only be Mac-Dougall. Her heart leapt, but try as she might she could see no sign of him in the quarter from which the coo-ee came several times in succession. Nor could she see the camp. It must still be hidden behind the trees.

Frantically she cupped her hands and tried to imitate the call. Her coo-ee was not loud but it carried farther than when she had called his name. Immediately there was an answering call from below. She called again, quaveringly, and he answered, but still there was no sign of him. Perhaps he hadn't heard her, she thought, and was just calling anyway. She decided to climb a little higher.

She scrambled up for only a short distance, almost at once reaching a ledge from which she could proceed no farther because of an outcrop of rocks blocking the way. The sun was hot on her uncovered head and she was terribly thirsty. As she looked down she suddenly felt dizzy and clung to the rock face behind her for support.

"Laur . . . a!"

This time she saw him, and a wave of indescribable joy washed over her. She managed to muster sufficient presence of mind and breath to shout, "Mac . . . up here!"

He had emerged from the trees almost at the same spot she had earlier, with Caesar running around sniffing the ground. The dog must have tracked her, she thought, breathing a heartfelt sigh of relief. She was found! She wasn't going to die of thirst or starve. Mac had found her.

She was so happy she did not even think about how angry he must be. She waved energetically and began to climb down to meet him. And that was when she found she couldn't make it. Climbing up had been difficult but she had managed it. Going down was nightmarish. All at once a feeling of nausea overtook her. It was not that she was at any great height, but as she looked down the whole scene began to swim before her eyes, and she had to lean back and close her eyes.

She heard MacDougall call anxiously, "Laura?" Suddenly her legs refused to move. Her knees were weak from running and the effort of climbing. Each time she tried to put one foot after the other she felt she was going to fall. She managed a few more steps and had to stop again. She looked down dizzily and saw MacDougall waiting ominously for her.

With a desperate little cry she called, "I . . . I can't . . . I'm stuck!" She closed her eyes as nausea swept over her again.

When she opened them he was coming up fast. "Laura . . . hang on . . . don't move . . . I'm coming . . . stay right where you are!"

Laura felt relief and at the same time deep shame. How he would deride her now! She would not let him, she thought. Let him be angry but she couldn't stand his scorn as well. She attempted to walk once more, but everything simply swirled around her, there was a moment of fractured light, then blackness as she crumpled into a heap between the rocks.

She came to a few moments later to find MacDougall cradling her head in his hands and saying anxiously, "Laura . . . are you all right?"

"I . . . I must have passed out," she gulped. "The heat . . ."

He nodded. His face was close to hers, his expression more concerned than angry. The wrath would come later, she thought miserably.

"We'd better get you down before you pass out again," he said, and gently raised her to her feet.

With his arm tightly encircling her waist, her head thankfully against his shoulder, they slowly negotiated the climb down. With Mac at her side, it was no longer an ordeal, and she felt ashamed for having succumbed to the wave of vertigo, something she had never suffered from before.

MacDougall did not speak, and Laura had no strength left

for words. When they reached level ground she pulled away from him, eager to show she no longer needed his support, but she staggered and he was obliged to catch her arm to steady her.

"I . . . I'm sorry," she murmured inadequately, "I . . . I . . ." She could find no words to apologize.

"Save your breath," he said rather curtly, and then, looking down into her white face, "You're in no fit state to walk back." Before she could protest, he had scooped her up in his arms and was marching off through the bush with swift purposeful strides, Caesar leading the way.

Laura had the feeling that to make an issue of it by struggling would only increase his impatience with her, so she submitted to being carried, and with her head against his shoulder, closed her eyes and tried to pretend that things were different, that this was not the last time she would ever be held in Robert MacDougall's arms, that he carried her in love, not impatient anger, and that he had forgiven her for her foolishness.

So, it was in a kind of blissful dreamy haze that she allowed him to carry her all the way back to the truck, as unaware of how far it was as she had been during her headlong dash away from it. It was only when he finally set her down in the shade of a tree near the truck that she realized what an unforgivable burden she had been. He was barely recovered from a bout of fever and he had been forced to search for her and bring her back. She looked up into his grim face, knowing she deserved everything he was bound to say to her.

"I . . . I'm sorry, Mac . . ." she faltered once more. "I . . . I shouldn't have said those things . . . I . . . I don't know what came over me. . . ."

His hand was still on her arm to steady her, and momentarily the pressure of his fingers tightened. There was an almost imperceptible twitch at the corner of his mouth, and he did not answer for a moment or two. At last he said in a clipped tone:

"You're lucky. Caesar's a pretty good tracker." Then he released her abruptly and added, "You'd better sit in the shade until you feel better. You've got a touch of sunstroke."

He strode off, but a moment later was back with a mug of cool water which she gratefully accepted. He said nothing and left her again.

Laura wanted desperately to run after him, apologize, even to make him angry again, anything rather than suffer the cold indifference he was now showing her, but she stayed where she was, clenching and unclenching her hands and taking deep breaths to keep control of her emotions.

After a few minutes she summoned the strength to walk rather shakily over to him. He was making tea. He looked up as she approached with the same cold stare as before.

"We might as well have an early lunch before we leave," he said.

"I'll get it . . ." Laura said at once.

"Are you feeling all right now?" His tone was considerate but cold.

"Mac . . . I want to say—" she began, but he cut her short.

"There's nothing to say. You were a bit overwrought, you ran off. . . ." He shrugged, dismissing it, but she could not.

"It was a stupid thing to do. I just didn't think. . . ."

His eyes were slate gray, impassive. "Not thinking in the bush has cost many a life," he said flatly.

"I know . . . and I'm sorry . . . I'm sorry for delaying you."

He stood up and looked at her expressionlessly. "Forget it, Laura. Something like this was bound to happen, I guess. That's why I don't take passengers. People get on each other's nerves. But it won't be long now. I'm afraid we're stuck with each other for a few more days whether we like it or not."

She turned away, unable to face him any longer. She helped prepare their lunch but neither of them had much appetite for the food. As they ate, Laura searched in vain for something to say that would clear the air and restore at least the moderately amicable relationship they had reached before last night. But all the time the memory of the long hours' vigil while he was feverish and delirious haunted her, as did the image of an unknown woman called Valerie. And she had foolishly imagined in a moment of egotistical madness that Mac's repressed desire had been for her, when all the time it had been for someone else, someone irretrievable whom he longed to hold in his arms.

At last he said, "Well, shall we make a start?"

She nodded. "I'll pack up."

He looked down at her in his slow enigmatic way, and for a moment his look was almost tender, and her heart turned over. He said, "Laura, I'm not angry. . . ."

She bit her lip. "Of course you are, and you've every right to be. I acted like a stupid fool. Just the way you expect someone like me to act. You should have gone off and left me, that's what I deserved."

For the first time he laughed. "Maybe . . . but even I am not that callous!" He added, in a puzzled tone, "What were you doing halfway up that cliff?"

"Trying to see where the camp was. I tried to climb a tree first, but that was too difficult. I thought if I could spot the truck I'd be all right, I'd find my way back."

He nodded and surprised her by saying, "Good thinking." The laughter had gone from his lips but still lurked in his eyes. "You are so impulsive, Laura, that's your trouble. You're always getting yourself into situations you can't get out of—like stowing away in the first place, and then wishing you hadn't."

"You were right, I have made a nuisance of myself," Laura said abjectly.

"Now, let's have no self-recrimination," he rebuked. "You won't get me to deny it by saying it yourself."

She drew in a sharp breath. "Oh, you're so hard, so cynical . . ." she blurted out.

He held up a restraining hand. "There you go again . . . but please don't run off because I just might not be so considerate next time. Come on, let's get going or we'll never make it to your brother by nightfall."

Suddenly the prospect of seeing Eric was even less attractive than before, and her apprehension increased. He wasn't going to think very highly of her when MacDougall told him about this little escapade.

"Come on, Laura. . . ." MacDougall bent and grasped her arm, raising her to her feet. He faced her with a quizzical smile, and suddenly something snapped inside her and she did the last thing she would have dreamed of doing had she had full control of herself. She just fell forward against him and buried her face against his broad chest, desperately wanting to weep, but managing to save herself from this final humiliation.

MacDougall did not push her away. His arms folded gently around her and he held her head against him as though she were a child to be comforted, his fingers stroking her hair soothingly. Emotion engulfed her and she was bursting to tell him that she loved him, but pride and her need to stifle her tears fortunately prevented it.

"Laura . . ." His voice was low, concerned. "Are you all right?"

She managed to gain control of herself, but when she tried to pull away he refused to let her go. "Mac . . . I'm sorry . . . I'm sorry . . ." she whispered over and over.

He soothed, "Shhh . . . don't go on about it. . . ."

She dared to look at him. "Let me go please. . . . I didn't mean to be all emotional and silly. I seem to have gone to pieces. . . ."

He loosened his grasp but held her at arm's length, giving her a long searching look before saying matter-of-factly, "I expect seeing the Prof will set you back on your feet. You've had a pretty grueling few days, and you've stood up to it pretty well considering, especially . . ." He paused and looked a trifle rueful, "especially as I haven't exactly made it easy for you."

She was astonished. "You couldn't help getting sick!"

He let a faint smile drift across his face. "That wasn't quite what I meant."

She stiffened, knowing full well now what he did mean. Not his abrasive and disparaging treatment of her, but his weakness in allowing himself to desire her. He seemed to think he owed her an apology for it. If only he knew, she thought, an apology was the last thing she wanted.

Chapter Ten

There was still an uneasy atmosphere between them when they set off again. Laura would have given anything for the past twenty-four hours not to have happened. As time went by she felt worse rather than better about her crazy dash into the bush that morning, and MacDougall's unexpectedly reasonable attitude only made her feel all the guiltier.

She had expected anger and derision, but he had been gentle and understanding. She sighed thinking about it. Understanding, yes, except that he did not and never would completely understand why she had acted that way. She glanced at him occasionally as the truck bumped on across rugged terrain, and just looking at him was like tightening iron bands on her heart.

His face was still a little paler than usual, but he seemed to have shaken off the fever quickly, and had regained his vigor despite the added strain and exertion of having to search for and rescue her. Sitting there, squeezed in beside him, with Caesar leaning heavily against her on the other side, Laura felt miserable and could not even look forward to seeing Eric.

It was midafternoon before MacDougall made any kind of remark, and when his voice finally broke the heavy silence, Laura gave a start.

"Not much farther now," he announced, glancing down at her just as she looked at him. He smiled. "Thirsty?"

"No . . ." She was, but was also determined not to be the cause of any further delay.

Nevertheless, he shortly stopped the truck in the shade of some trees. "I could do with a drink," he said, "and so could Caesar." He mopped his brow and jumped out.

Laura let Caesar out, and when MacDougall offered it she too accepted a mug of water from the water bag that swung behind the truck. She walked a few steps away, half turning from him, and then found he had followed her.

"Laura . . ." His voice was hesitant and tinged with anxiety. He seemed a different MacDougall somehow, but she stiffened at his approach, warily.

"Yes . . ."

"Laura . . . stop worrying about what happened this morning. It doesn't matter. I'm not angry with you. . . ."

"Why not?" She flashed a look at him. "You ought to be. . . ."

His hand dropped lightly onto her shoulder, and his touch sent shock waves through her. She wanted to bury her head against his chest and let him hold her close again, and it required a supreme effort of will not to give in to the impulse to do just that.

He turned her around to face him with the pressure of his one hand. "Laura . . . there's something I've been trying to recall . . . about last night. I'm not sure whether it was a dream or not . . . but you were there saying something— something terribly important . . . only I can't remember. . . ."

Her eyes flickered in panic. He mustn't remember! He simply mustn't! She searched his face anxiously. Perhaps he had already remembered and was just trying to make her admit it. His deep gray eyes were gentler than she had ever known them, but clouded with uncertainty as he questioned her.

She took a deep breath. "Mac . . . I really don't know what you can mean. I . . . I didn't say anything important—at least only when I was trying to get you to tell me which bottle contained the right medication. I think you must have been dreaming . . . you were very delirious and . . . and a bit incoherent."

A smile flickered briefly across his lips. "I confess I do wonder what I was raving on about. I can't remember a thing."

She rushed in with reassurance. "Nothing, Mac, nothing much at all that I could make any sense of. It was all very disjointed." She added, "And in any case I was too worried to try and make sense of it. Besides, what people say when they're delirious is private, not for eavesdropping on." She made herself look at him steadily, willing him to believe her, but by the way he looked at her she was not sure he did.

After a moment he slipped his arm across her shoulders and said briskly, "Let's get moving. We'll be there in an hour or two."

There was no positive reason for it, but the tension between them seemed to have eased a little after the stop for a drink. MacDougall chatted casually with Laura from time to time, and she, after a while, suddenly regained the excited anticipation she had felt from the start as she realized that very shortly she would actually be seeing Eric at last.

This did not prevent, however, the strain and lack of sleep of the previous night from finally catching up with her, and lulled by the sound of the truck's engine, and the warmth in the cabin, she dozed off.

She was awakened abruptly when MacDougall blew the horn loudly. Her head was resting against his shoulder and she sat bolt upright guiltily, in time to see an aborigine emerging from the bush just ahead of them. He was carrying a kangaroo carcass over his shoulder. Laura flinched a little at the sight of the dead animal, and MacDougall called out as the truck drew level, "G'day, Charlie!"

"G'day, Mac," replied Charlie, giving Laura a toothy grin. "We bin wondering where you got to, but we reckoned you'd catch up with us soon."

"We got the Prof's note," said MacDougall. "Want to hop on for a ride? Plenty of room at the back."

The truck started off again and MacDougall said to Laura, "Civilization has its advantages. Charlie never says no to a lift!"

"Is he one of Eric's tribe?" she asked.

"Yep. And my best stockman."

Laura turned to him, surprised. "He works for you?"

He nodded. "Most of them work for me at Nilla Nilla. They have a permanent camp there, but now and then they go walkabout. We don't see them for a few weeks or so and then they drift back again. They're staying in the bush longer this time because of the Prof."

"Don't they mind him studying their ways?"

"Apparently not. They're quite proud of the fact. They like yarning away about legends and customs and all that sort of thing. They show him how to live off the land in all sorts of conditions. And he's a very unobtrusive scientist, living exactly the way they do so he's almost one of them."

"Who does the work on the station when they aren't there?" Laura asked.

He shrugged. "We manage. There are other employees, and anyway this long jaunt was organized specially quite a while back to coincide with a slack time."

"I see. It was you who organized it all for Eric?"

He nodded. "More or less."

The truck rumbled on and Laura was beginning to wonder if they were ever going to find the place they were supposed to be heading for, when all at once they squeezed through a narrow pass between high rocky cliffs and emerged into a valley which came as a shock to Laura.

Having become used to the blue-gray monotony of the gum trees, drab-foliaged scrub and barren hillsides, she was unprepared for the startling contrasts in this veritable oasis of a valley. It was quite unlike where they had camped last night. The rocky cliffs enclosing the valley were higher, the vegetation much greener and lusher than anywhere she had so far been. There were large pools of sparkling water surrounded by the dazzling smooth white trunks of ghost gums and edged with dense undergrowth. Laura could not help a gasp of surprise.

MacDougall shot her a smiling glance. "Different, isn't it? It must have amazed the first explorer who came upon it, after trudging for days probably across the desert."

"Like finding the Garden of Eden," said Laura, with a smile.

"No Adam and Eve, but plenty of snakes!" said MacDougall, and when Laura shuddered, he added with a laugh, "Don't worry, you probably won't see any."

"I hope not!" she exclaimed.

The truck rattled and bumped along until the valley widened out, and all at once Laura spotted a dozen or so men, women and children running toward them waving. Half a dozen dogs barked at their heels, and among the black bodies Laura saw there was one less dark, with a red beard and a bush hat squashed down over his unruly hair.

"Eric!" she exclaimed, and a rush of emotion choked her.

MacDougall braked and as the truck came to a halt it was immediately surrounded by the welcoming party. Caesar went wild as Laura opened the door to let him out and instantly began cavorting excitedly with the dogs which bounded up to greet him like old friends, which no doubt they were.

Eric, not noticing Laura at first as she stepped down on the right side, greeted MacDougall, who grinned and said, "Brought a surprise for you this trip, Prof." He indicated Laura with an outstretched hand.

"A surprise?" The professor, looking around, saw Laura standing there smiling at him. His face became a picture of astonishment. "Good God, *Laura!*" For a moment he looked as though he did not believe his own eyes, then he held out his arms. "Laura . . . what in heaven's name . . . ?"

She rushed into his arms. "Eric . . . at last . . . oh, I thought we'd never get here." She hugged him happily. "And you recognized me!"

He held her away from him, looking at her. "Of course I recognized you! You haven't changed much."

She pretended to pout. "I've grown up!"

He gave her a quick hug. "Oh, yes, you've done that, I daresay, but you're still the same Laura." He looked at her again and said, "And if anything, even more beautiful!"

She was embarrassed and blushed. "Oh really . . ."

He grinned. "Well, not bad-looking . . . eh, Mac?" He winked at MacDougall, who stood discreetly to one side, a half-smile on his face as he filled his pipe and lit it while exchanging remarks with the chattering aborigines.

"Considering the last few days, not bad . . ." he drawled laconically.

Professor Fairchild slipped his arm firmly around Laura's shoulders. "Now, tell me, what on earth are you doing here? And how did you manage to persuade Mac to bring you?"

MacDougall broke in, "Just so we all know where the responsibility lies, she didn't persuade me, Prof. I wouldn't have anything to do with it. She stowed away!"

Laura's color deepened, and Eric stared at her. "In the truck?"

She nodded and caught MacDougall's eye, which mocked her.

"You little devil!" exclaimed the professor. He gave her an affectionate shake. "Come along, you're going to tell me all about this right from the beginning. I'm very flattered, but I really can't imagine why you took it into your head to come out here to see me." He shook his head in wonderment. "But, Laura, in any case, it's wonderful! I'm delighted to see you, even if I am somewhat dismayed to find you grown into a headstrong young woman. Stowing away!"

"Now, don't you start doing the big brother act with me," said Laura, laughing, as they walked toward the camp. "I've had a tough enough time with MacDougall."

The professor glanced at the tall Australian who walked beside them and his eyes narrowed suspiciously. Laura hastened to add, "Oh, he's been the perfect gentleman, Eric, I assure you, and he has put up with me exceedingly well."

Eric looked at her with a touch of pride, and still in disbelief. "I can't believe you're actually here," he said. "Extraordinary!"

It did not take Laura long to tell her brother the whole

story. She related the sad details of her mother's death, and the salutary experience of Romilly's defection, and explained why she had suddenly decided to come to Australia to see him. It was not easy to explain her feelings of emptiness, the lack of direction she had felt, the need to find herself again. It was asking too much, she realized, to expect him to understand, but she talked about it just the same and Eric was sympathetic and did seem to appreciate her feelings.

For Laura it was simply good to be able to unburden at least part of her emotional tangle into a sympathetic ear. She could not, of course, tell him how she felt about MacDougall. She described the trip in the truck only sketchily and hoped that Mac would not take too much delight in regaling Eric with her shortcomings, particularly her foolish behavior that morning.

They were still talking, sitting by the largest water hole near the camp when dusk came down softly over the valley, after a flaming sunset.

"The trouble with you, Laura," Eric said, taking her hand and patting it in a brotherly way, "is that you've always let other people push you around. No, to be quite blunt about it—your mother dominated you." He smiled wryly at her. "Just as she did your father."

Laura sighed. "I know. . . ."

"And the time has come," Eric went on firmly, but not unkindly, "for you to stand on your own two feet. You are quite capable of doing it. In fact you are *already* doing it! You've come all this way to see me for advice and support, when in fact you don't need it. You can manage your own life, I feel certain."

Laura felt foolish, and again wished she had not given in to the crazy impulse to come. "I suppose so . . ." she admitted reluctantly. "Oh, Eric, I'm sorry, bothering you like this. I shouldn't have come, but . . . well, I suppose I just needed someone to say it to me, someone to bolster my confidence, and since you are my only close relative, wanting to see you became a sort of obsession."

"Laura, love, don't think I'm saying you shouldn't have come," said Eric at once. "I think it was very brave and

141

enterprising of you to do so, and I'm delighted to see you. I do understand why you wanted to. You were feeling utterly bereft. Even though you didn't get on well with your mother, she was a prop, security, and perhaps Romilly was too, in a way. You leaned on them, and naturally you felt unstable when the props were taken away."

"So I looked for another prop," Laura said sheepishly. "And I picked on you."

He laughed softly. "And what a poor old prop I am proving to be. Oh dear, Laura, I'm afraid I'm not going to be much help to you. I suspect there is nothing I can say that you don't already know. I think you've learned your own answers already."

Laura looked at him fondly. "Yes, I think I have . . . some of them anyway. Mac said we have to solve our own problems and he's right." She reflected ruefully that in the past few days she had indeed learned a great deal about herself. She said abruptly, "Eric . . . Eric, I don't want to go back to England. I've given it a lot of thought and I want to make a fresh start. I want to give all that up."

He looked startled. "Give what up?"

She shrugged. "Everything, the whole way of life, the beauty business."

"Has MacDougall been slinging off at you?" He smiled slyly.

Laura colored. "It's not that . . . it's just that I didn't ever want to be a beautician—I don't think. The trouble was I didn't know what I wanted, so Mother pushed me into it. Oh, it's a perfectly respectable and useful occupation, I'm not sneering at it, but I . . ." She paused, hardly daring to suggest what was in her mind, especially since MacDougall had already thrown cold water on it. She took a deep breath and rushed on recklessly, "Eric, I thought . . . well, I thought maybe I could help you with your work. . . ." She looked at him anxiously, fearful he would burst out laughing as Mac had.

He did not. He looked astonished, and stared at her nonplussed for a moment before he said with a slow shake of his head, "I'm sorry, Laura, but that would be impossible."

He looked distressed. "I would like to say yes, but I can't. Have you considered how I live for a start? Here, there and everywhere, living like a hobo most of the time?"

"I wouldn't mind roughing it," Laura said eagerly. "I've been living pretty rough these past few days."

He chuckled. "No, Laura. A few days is one thing, trailing around after me is another. I couldn't let you do that."

"Please," she begged. "Surely I could be useful to you."

An expression of pain crossed his kindly face. "Laura, love," he said reluctantly after a moment, "I don't think you quite understand. I'm a loner, and I work alone. I like it that way. I'm sorry to be so blunt but that's how it is."

She saw her mistake and wished she'd had the wit to see it before. "Of course . . . I'm an idiot, Eric, to have even suggested it. I didn't think it through properly. If you'd wanted someone to tag along you'd have engaged an assistant by now, or gotten married. You wouldn't want your kid sister anyway."

He frowned. "Laura . . . I didn't mean it to sound so unkind. It's not that I'm not fond of you, but it's just that I'm not accustomed to . . . well, responsibilities."

"I'd be more than that," she said dully, "I'd be a liability." She drew a deep breath and let it out slowly. "I've embarrassed you even mentioning it. Eric . . . I'm sorry."

He squeezed her hand. "It was a very commendable idea but just not practical. Besides, you're not even trained in anthropology."

"Mac said it was a crazy idea," she said. "And of course he was right, but I just wanted to be near someone I knew . . . to belong somewhere again . . . I felt so . . . so . . ." Words suddenly failed her.

"Lonely?" suggested Eric.

She nodded.

A smile creased his deeply tanned and freckled face. "Laura, love, you don't need a selfish, self-centered older brother with a passion for losing himself in the wilderness, you need someone to fall in love with. Love is the greatest cure for loneliness and lack of purpose."

Laura bit her lip. Maybe he was right, but only if the person

143

you loved loved you too. If they didn't then the loneliness was worse and there was hurt as well. She had had plenty of experience of that. There had been Romilly . . . and now there was MacDougall.

She said lightly, "But unfortunately one can't fall in love for convenience!"

Eric laughed. "Perhaps not! So we'll have to think of something else for you to do in the meantime."

"You really don't have to feel responsible for me," Laura insisted hastily. "I really am quite capable of looking after myself. I'd no right to foist myself on you. I'll work something out."

"Now don't start overdoing the independence," Eric reproved. "I'm just thinking. . . ." He smiled at her fondly. "Laura, you can't turn up out of the blue like this and then just skip off with MacDougall back to town and out of my life again."

"I shouldn't have barged into it in the first place."

"But you have, and I'm glad. I'm not letting you go without at least seeing a bit more of you first, and we're going to keep track of each other in the future, especially if you decide to stay in Australia. I don't spend all my time here, but I do have a base of sorts in Sydney."

"Eric, you really don't have to . . ." Laura felt now that she had made herself an awkward burden.

He said firmly, "I know I don't have to, but I want to! Now, stop feeling guilty and listen to me. I've almost finished my work here, and I was going to tell Mac I'd probably want to go back with him next trip. Now, here's my idea. Down in Sydney I have permanent digs with a nice motherly lady called Mrs. Lindsay. She will love to meet you, and I suggest you go straight to her and I'll join you as soon as I can."

"But, Eric . . ." Laura protested.

"But nothing. Elsie will be delighted to have you. She's always got room for one more, and she's just the kind of person to help you settle yourself into a new job and a new life. You can have a good look around Sydney and see how you like it. If you decide to stay there, then we'll be able to see each other from time to time."

Laura felt a sense of security stealing over her such as she had not felt for a long time. "I could get a flat," she said eagerly, "and it could be your base too." She added, "Are you sure Mrs. Lindsay won't mind?"

"I'm a hundred percent sure," said her brother. "I'll write her a note to explain." He grinned mischievously. "Although, I'm not sure MacDougall will approve!"

"And what will MacDougall not approve?" inquired a familiar gravelly voice, and suddenly he was there, looking down at them, his gray eyes on Laura with a coolly questioning look.

She felt embarrassed. There was a faint innuendo in Eric's remark. Her brother explained the situation, and Mac listened impassively, then drawled, "It sounds an excellent plan. You'll enjoy Sydney, Laura."

"I'm sure I shall." She was unable for a moment to meet his gaze, feeling already the wrench of leaving him, knowing it would be no wrench for him.

He said, "I came to tell you there's going to be a dance festival—a corroboree—tonight in our honor.

Laura was thrilled. She felt a little less heavyhearted after her talk with Eric. There was some shape to the future at last. They walked back toward the camp where the aborigines were busily painting their bodies ready for the performance. Laura was fascinated.

MacDougall turned to her with a faintly mocking smile and said, "Maybe you could give them a few tips on makeup, Laura!"

She ignored his remark, but he added a further jibe, "You'll be expected to eat everything offered to you tonight or you'll risk offending them."

Laura shot him a haughty look. "I'm sure I shall enjoy any new experience!"

Later she saw him watching her with a half-smile on his lips, mocking her again, as she valiantly kept her word and ate everything the aborigines gave her, even if she was not always sure what it was. Once she caught his eye and it was not mocking but idly speculative again, and she wondered what he was thinking.

After the meal the corroboree began. Laura watched, entranced, never having seen anything like it before. It was not one of the secret ceremonies, Eric told her, but a collection of ritual dances and mimes which strangers and women were permitted to see.

The dancers' bodies were intricately painted and some wore feathered headdresses or the skins of animals. They performed mime dances that imitated the movements of the kangaroo, the emu, the snake, the frog and many others. One man played the didgeridoo, others chanted songs, and the primitive rhythms echoed and reechoed across the steeply sided valley.

Finally the dancers invited their guests to join in. Laura, intoxicated by the strange sounds and hypnotic rhythms, the weird chants, leapt up eagerly and danced with them energetically. For a few minutes she was no longer Laura Fairchild but one of them as her bare feet pounded in the dust and the primeval music drummed in her ears.

The chanting was still reverberating in her head when she finally dragged her sleeping bag out of the truck and placed it, as she was now accustomed to doing, on the right side. The moon was rising, not red and savage tonight, but mellow and golden. Laura, gazing at it as it hung like a giant pumpkin over the silhouetted hills, felt an extraordinary peace and contentment, and as she stood there, drinking in the beauty of the night, she was startled suddenly to find MacDougall beside her.

"Did you enjoy the entertainment?" he inquired casually, leaning against the truck idly, drawing on his pipe, totally relaxed.

Laura's heart was racing at his nearness. The aroma of his pipe tobacco drifted to her, mingled with the woodsmoke from the campfires and the faint perfumes of the bush.

"Very much," she answered, drawing a little away from him, afraid that even her tone of voice might give away her feelings.

How she was going to endure the drive back to Camel Creek alone with him, she did not know. It would be agony being forced to sit close beside him in the truck, all the while longing for him to hold her in his arms. But he would never do that again. He had made it abundantly clear that those moments when they had both been overwhelmed by the power of their own feelings were nothing more than that— moments of impulse that meant nothing. She had nothing to fear from him, he had made that clear too. It was just as well, she thought ruefully, because she suspected that it was her own power to resist that would be in question, not his.

"Another new experience for you, the corroboree," he observed.

"Yes." She glanced at him, smoking contentedly, a man completely at ease in his chosen environment, a man at home in this wild and unpredictable country, as much a part of it as the jagged red hills, the ghost gums and the aborigines. She said, "I loved it. I got quite carried away!"

He turned to her with a half-smile that held no trace of his usual mockery. "I'll say you did!"

"Did I do wrong?" she demanded guiltily.

He chuckled. "No! They loved you for joining in so wholeheartedly, for really enjoying yourself in such an uninhibited way, not just pretending. They respect people who don't patronize them." His enigmatic gray eyes roved slowly across her face. "Many quite genuinely kind people still patronize them. They resent that."

"I . . . I didn't consciously not . . . do anything," she faltered.

He took his pipe out of his mouth and knocked the ashes out on the side of the truck, then stowed it in the pocket of his shirt. He seemed in no hurry to turn in yet. After a moment or two of searching scrutiny, he took a step closer to her and suddenly tilted her chin with a firm hand so that she was forced to meet his gaze without flinching.

"No, you were absolutely natural," he murmured, his eyes still fixed on her face. In a low voice he went on, "You know, Laura, you don't need makeup to be beautiful. When your face lights up . . ." His own face hovered so close to hers that she thought for one wild moment that he was going to kiss her, and she longed for him to, for his lips to meet hers with the same exquisite tenderness and passion as before, so that every fiber of her being was roused in response to the slightest caress.

Tenderness was in his eyes now, thinly veiling the desire she knew he felt, and she knew she only had to make the slightest move and he would hold her close and turn the agony of longing into a transport of delight.

We belong together, she thought recklessly, and, heedless of the consequences, she knew she could hold back no longer. She must tell him she loved him. . . . But even as the words were forming, his eyes suddenly narrowed and became hard, his mouth gave a bitter little twist and the tenderness vanished, the desire faded and he looked at her as though he despised her. The look hurt so deeply she could not speak. She saw the futility of it, and was grateful that she had been saved from humiliation. As he stepped back, his hand falling to his side, a shudder ran through her.

He said roughly, "The trouble with hothouse plants is, they don't transplant into the bush. They flourish for a while and then wither and die. The only way to save them is to send them back to where they came from." He was watching the moon and seemed unaware of her.

Laura, shaken, managed to say lightly, "That's rather cryptic. May I ask what it means?"

His head jerked around in surprise that she was still there, it seemed. "I was thinking aloud," he said crushingly.

She felt nettled. "I suppose you consider that I am a hothouse plant that could never survive in the bush," she said.

He glanced at her, a swift encompassing glance. "The Prof isn't willing to take the chance."

Laura bit her lip. "It . . . it would be rather impractical. . . ."

"You'll be glad," said MacDougall confidently. "You'll be glad he turned you down. You'll find yourself a nice comfortable little pad in Sydney, if you don't change your mind and go back to London, and you'll soon have a good job in a beauty parlor again. You're a city girl, Laura. Life in the bush wouldn't suit you, not even a slightly more civilized version than Eric's."

"Such as?"

He shrugged, then laughed. "Well, barmaid at the Camel Creek Hotel for instance!"

She felt even more annoyed with him. "I might be more adaptable than you think!"

"You might," he conceded, "but I doubt it." He took out his pipe and began to refill it, and seemed to drift far away into private thoughts, ignoring her and yet apparently in no hurry to leave her.

Laura, on edge now, all the peace and contentment shattered by this enigmatic man who had the power to turn her whole being upside down, said sharply, "Well, I don't think this conversation is getting us very far, and actually I'm rather tired. I imagine you must be feeling a bit exhausted after your bout of fever too; so hadn't we better turn in?"

He looked startled, as though her words had wrenched him back to reality from some distant corner of his consciousness.

"Sorry . . . it's late of course . . . and you must be worn-out." He touched her shoulder briefly with his hand. "Good night, Laura."

Her lip trembled. Now she had asked him to go, she wished she had not, even though just by being there he churned her emotions painfully.

"Good night, Mac . . ." she murmured softly. "Sleep well."

He strode away, a dark shadow vanishing around the other side of the truck, and presently she heard the faint sounds as he climbed into his sleeping bag. When she settled down in hers, she felt suddenly the full impact of her loneliness. She had come to Australia because she had felt lost and lonely, but now she felt even more achingly so, and all because of a tall, blond, gray-eyed enigmatic man called MacDougall.

Chapter Eleven

Laura rose early next morning, expecting that MacDougall would want to depart as soon as possible. She would have liked more time with Eric but she knew it was not possible. MacDougall had made it quite clear that their visit would be brief. That had been one of his reasons for refusing to take her in the first place, that it just wasn't worth it.

But it had been, she reflected, as she rolled up her sleeping bag and stowed it in the truck. She didn't regret coming to see Eric, and talking to him. The only regrettable thing was that she had foolishly fallen in love with MacDougall. But that surely would be temporary. It would fade quickly once she was away from him, just as Romilly had quickly faded from her mind and she had realized she had never really loved him. But her thoughts lacked conviction, and all the more so when she saw MacDougall striding toward the truck. She could see beyond him the spiral of smoke from the campfire where dark figures were moving about in the gray dawn light.

"I suppose you want to get away soon," she said, with a note of regret. "I'd better say good-bye to Eric."

He took his pipe out of his mouth and said diffidently, "We're stopping here for today."

It was a very surprising announcement for him to make, and Laura was touched by his consideration. "You don't have to be held up just because of me . . . and Eric . . ." she said.

He raised his eyebrows. "What makes you think I'm stopping for you? After my bout of fever, I thought a day's relaxation might be a sensible course."

Laura wished she had not expressed the thought. She should have known he wouldn't put himself out for her. "Sorry," she said shortly, "it is a good idea for you to rest up a bit." She felt crushed.

"You'll be able to have a swim," he said, "and gather your strength for the rest of the ordeal."

Laura did not reply. His sarcasm hurt, and she had no wish to bicker with him. She walked over to the campfire where she could see Eric.

He said, "Mac's decided to have a day off so we two can chin-wag for a bit longer. Good of him."

Laura smiled wryly. "Yes, very good." Her tone made the professor glance at her sharply.

Later in the morning Laura decided to have her swim. With so many half-naked bodies around she felt less self-conscious about stripping completely especially as at the time there were only the women and children at the water hole.

The children were delighted to have a new companion to show off to, and there was a great deal of animated horseplay and laughter as Laura larked with them in the water. Jumping about and swimming amid all the black shining bodies, she felt very conscious of her insipid white skin, but she felt a freedom she had never experienced before. She felt totally relaxed and for a time all her problems were forgotten.

It was only when she glanced up and saw Eric and MacDougall approaching that her problems returned, and with them her inhibitions. Hurriedly she scrambled out onto the rock that overhung the water hole and put on her shirt and slacks, heedless of her wet skin. She was however premature, for the men did not come to the water hole then, but disappeared from her view.

As the women and children were all clambering out now, anyway, Laura stayed where she was and stretched out on the rock, which was sheltered from the blazing sun by a canopy of leaves that barely stirred in the hot air. As she gazed at the fragmented blue sky through the leaves, a strange feeling stole over her. She felt as though she was melting into the rock, being absorbed by it, almost as though she knew what it was like to be a rock—a part of the landscape, as Harry Bambridge the old prospector had seemed that day as they were leaving him, as MacDougall had seemed that night silhouetted against the moon, as Eric had seemed last night squatting in the dust taking his turn playing the didgeridoo.

Laura smiled to herself. She had been listening to too many of Eric's stories. Last night, while they were eating, he had related some of the aboriginal myths about spirits that inhabited the trees and rocks and animals. It was a strange and beautiful country, she thought suddenly, and it gave you fanciful ideas.

"Well, lizard, enjoying yourself?"

Laura started, as Eric flopped down beside her. He was alone and she was glad.

She laughed. "I feel a bit like one!" She stretched. "This is sheer bliss. Eric, I know you think I'm mad, but I'm glad I came."

"And not just because of me," he remarked dryly. "I've been a bit of a wet blanket really, haven't I? I've been thinking about it, Laura, but I really can't see . . ."

"Eric, please . . ." she protested. "Don't start feeling—responsible! I shall wish I hadn't come. It's been a tremendous experience for me—and a help. Really."

"You're a plucky kid," he said, but it didn't irk as much as it did when MacDougall referred to her as a child. Eric laughed. "Taking on MacDougall takes some nerve!"

"He certainly makes it clear he hasn't much time for women," said Laura.

"He's been quite complimentary about you. You've earned your keep by the sound of it. He told me about the truck getting bogged, and how you drove it out. He was pretty impressed by that."

Laura felt a rush of relief. But of course even Mac would be too tactful to tell Eric that he despised his sister and couldn't wait to see the last of her.

"He thinks I'm just a spoiled brat," she said.

Eric grimaced. "Partly my fault, I suppose. I did sound off once about Lillian . . . you know how we knocked sparks off each other, and I didn't approve . . . well, that's all water under the bridge. Of course I didn't know he'd ever meet you. It was only natural, I suppose, he assumed you were cast in the same mold as her." He smiled at her affectionately, "But you're not, bless you." He paused and then apologized, "I'm sorry, I shouldn't talk about Lillian. She was your mother."

Laura raised her eyes to his. "And I knew her, Eric. You don't have to pretend! She was all you despised her for, and I'm not surprised you couldn't stand to see what she was doing to Dad, but I loved her in a funny sort of way. She wasn't malicious, just superficial. I can see why Dad fell for her."

Eric said soberly, "To tell you the truth, Laura, so could I. I've often wondered if perhaps I wasn't a little in love with her myself. She was more my age after all!"

Laura laughed. "Can you see her trailing around the Outback with you?"

"No. I've never thought it would be fair to expect any woman to do that. And I'm too selfish anyway to share my life with anyone. A bachelor I shall probably remain to the end of my days."

"Like MacDougall," she said, and then added, "but he was married once, of course. . . ."

Eric looked surprised. "He told you about it?"

"No. Mrs. Gordon at Margaret Springs mentioned it . . . was her name Valerie, Eric?"

"Yes . . . yes, it was. . . ."

"What happened?" Laura could not help herself.

"She died."

"Oh!" Laura was shocked. She had thought of Valerie as alive, as someone who had let MacDougall down, not as dead. She felt ashamed of hating the unknown woman, and knew she had been foolish to let her imagination run away with her.

After a moment, Eric said, "He never talks about it . . . he's a very private person."

Laura sensed his reluctance to break what he perhaps felt was a confidence. Although she was anxious to know anything at all about MacDougall, she said, "You don't have to tell me . . . if you'd rather not."

Her brother looked at her steadily. "Are you falling in love with him?"

"No!" She averted her eyes.

The professor chuckled. "That denial was too vehement, my dear. Look at me! Be truthful. . . ."

Laura forced herself to meet his eyes. She knew hers would give her away. Eric could read her like a book. He had always been perceptive where she was concerned, even when she was a little girl.

She dropped her gaze to her hands splayed on the rock. There were still vestiges of nail varnish on her fingernails. Her hands looked rough and unkempt, but the sight of them did not dismay her as it once would have done.

"I know it is not likely to be reciprocated," she whispered. She clenched her fingers into fists and banged them on the rock. "I didn't mean it to happen. He hasn't given me the slightest encouragement—he despises me and makes sure I know it. . . ."

"He's good-looking . . . an attractive man. . . ." murmured her brother.

Laura looked at him miserably. "It's so much more than that . . . he's . . . he's so much a—*man*. Oh, I can't explain, Eric . . . it's just that I never met anyone like him before. . . ."

"The unattainable is always a challenge," Eric said bluntly.

Laura was silent. Was that all it was, a challenge? Did she imagine she loved MacDougall simply because MacDougall was unattainable?

"Perhaps that's all it is," she said wearily. "It doesn't matter anyhow. In a few days I'll be gone and I'll never see him again."

After a moment's silence, Eric said, "Perhaps you do have a right to know why he is unattainable. It might help you to understand him."

Laura looked up expectantly, and he went on, "He may have told you he owns a cattle station. . . ."

"Yes. I can't understand why he leaves the running of it to a manager while he does this run and other odd contracting jobs. He obviously doesn't need the money, and I don't suppose it's very lucrative anyway."

"There's a very good reason," said Eric. "Let me go back a few years to when Mac's parents were alive. He was educated in the city and traveled around the world for a year or two afterwards. His father didn't want him to bury himself in the Outback unless he really wanted to. After he came back from his wanderings he took a job in Sydney for a while and it was there that he met Valerie Wiseman, an aspiring actress.

"They were to be married, but Mac's father died and he had to come home. He ended up staying, not just for his mother's sake, although that must have been part of it. He just felt this was where he belonged after all. Meanwhile Valerie had been offered a chance to go overseas, so she went, and she stayed, and eventually the engagement was broken off."

"But he married her," broke in Laura.

Eric shook his head. "Not then. A couple of years after they broke off their engagement she came back to make a film, set in the Australian Outback. She had evidently told the film company about Mac, and suggested they persuade him to let them film on his property. Naturally, as a result, he and Valerie saw a lot of each other again. His mother had died by then and he was no doubt rather lonely. The romance flared up again, and as Valerie's career was not going too well despite the film—in which she only had a fairly minor role, I gather—she evidently decided it would be more attractive to be a station owner's wife than a failed actress. It was afterwards that she dropped the bombshell. She had no intention of living at Nilla Nilla. She wanted to live in the city, and expected Mac to put in a manager, or sell up, and do the same. He refused. There were rows about it when she went away from time to time. Then, when she was pregnant, he thought she would settle down after the baby was born, but she didn't. She was worse and worse and began to go away frequently. I'm afraid she and your mother had a great deal in common. It was when Mac told me about Valerie in a rare burst of confidence one day that I told him about Lillian, as a sort of consolation, though nothing could really be that. . . . Well, anyway, there were continual rows and reconciliations, until finally she delivered an ultimatum, the station or her. He told her to go to hell, and she stalked out taking the baby. She took a four-wheel drive and went like a bat out of hell, in the middle of a storm. She was caught in a flash flood before she was even off the property. Both she and the child were drowned."

Laura felt the tears welling up in her eyes. She was seeing MacDougall, three nights ago, watching the water burst down the creek bed. She knew now what the terrible anguish he had gone through in that moment signified. She knew why he had shouted out "The water . . . the water!" in his delirium.

"How terrible," she breathed, in a choked voice. "Oh, Eric . . . how dreadful it must have been for him."

"He blamed himself, of course. He believed he should have gone after her, stopped her leaving. But he was angry, at the end of his tether with her, and lost his temper. Anyway, how could he have known that would happen? He believes he should have done what she wanted, not been stubborn and selfish. He hasn't exactly said so but that's why he goes to the station as little as possible. He can't bring himself to cut himself off completely because he loves the place, but he can't bear to be there with his memories."

"It explains a lot," said Laura slowly.

Eric patted her hand. "Try not to get hurt, Laura, love."

"No . . ." she said ruefully. But she was already hurt, and what Eric had told her only made her love MacDougall more.

"You've only known him for a few days," her brother said.

"I know. But I've been with him constantly in that time. It's the same as seeing someone for a couple of hours every day for much much longer." Time was unimportant anyway, she thought. You could fall in love in a minute, an hour, a day

156

or a week, or it could take a year. There was no fixed rule. She recalled the morning she had peered out of her bedroom at the Camel Creek hotel and he had been coming along the passage, a towel wrapped around his waist, his hair still damp from the shower. It may have even happened then.

"He loves her so much," she said resignedly. "When he was delirious, Eric, he kept calling her name and begging her not to leave him."

Eric said softly, "Poor little Laura. I wish I could help. I'm not much use as a shoulder to cry on."

Laura sat up and hugged her knees, determined not to be maudlin. "Don't let's talk about it anymore."

He grimaced. "All right. I'll change the subject. If you're going to give up being a beautician, what else do you think you'll do?"

She shrugged. "I've no idea." She added with a confidence she did not yet feel, "Something will turn up I expect."

"What really interests you, Laura?" Eric persisted.

She heaved a sigh. "I don't know . . . or perhaps I do. Eric, I know this sounds silly, especially today, but I don't really think I'm cut out to be a career girl. I'm a homebody at heart." She laughed self-deprecatingly. "Doesn't that sound horribly unimaginative! But what I really want to do, I think, is get married and look after a family." She blushed deeply after this confession and waited for him to scoff.

He didn't. "That's not an ambition to be ashamed of," he said seriously. "You were always a loving girl, Laura." He chuckled. "A girl like you would have suited Mac better than Valerie. She was totally wrong for a man like him."

"But he still loves her nevertheless," said Laura bleakly, and thought, and he despises me because he believes I am like her. But I wouldn't be, she added to herself fiercely—I wouldn't be if he would only give me the chance.

"He's just afraid to make the same mistake twice," said Eric soberly, "and I suppose one can't blame him."

"Well, don't for goodness sake tell him my secret ambition," Laura said, with an attempt at lightheartedness. "He might drive off in the night without me, terrified out of his wits!"

157

Eric laughed too. "More likely he wouldn't believe you! But who knows, Laura, the next few days might change matters. When he realizes that he won't be seeing you again. . . ."

Laura knew he was just trying to be kind. "That will be a relief to him, Eric, and don't imagine anything else."

"You two can certainly chin-wag!" MacDougall was suddenly standing beside them, appearing as if on cue. He smiled enigmatically at Laura and then turned to Eric. "Well, are you going to show me those cave paintings, Prof?"

"Sure." Eric stood up. "Laura? You'd like to see them too, wouldn't you?"

Laura jumped up and slipped her feet into her sandals. MacDougall glanced down at them. After her mad dash through the bush they were in even worse condition than before, but nevertheless still holding together.

"It's quite a climb, isn't it?" he said to Eric.

The professor nodded and also glanced at Laura's feet. For a moment she was afraid Mac was going to tell him how she had become stuck halfway up the cliff yesterday morning and had passed out, but he did not. Eric said, "There's a reasonable path, if Laura thinks she can manage it."

MacDougall looked at her questioningly, a flicker of concern flashing briefly across his face.

"I'd like to come," she said, adding to her brother, "Are you sure they won't mind outsiders looking?" But she was the only outsider really, she thought. Mac was almost as much one of them as Eric.

"They told me it's all right," Eric assured her. "They trust you not to reveal where the cave is."

MacDougall smiled teasingly at Laura. "I expect you'd find it impossible to guide a press party to this spot anyway!"

She shot him a cool look and said nothing. It was true of course. She had no idea where in all this vast Outback she was.

Eric consulted his watch. "I suggest we eat first."

After lunch, which Laura assisted the aboriginal women to prepare, she and Eric and MacDougall left the camp, guided by one of the aborigines, the man Charlie to whom they had given a lift.

As they were leaving, MacDougall said to Laura in a low tone, "Are you sure you'll be all right? It'll be hot. . . ."

"I'll be all right," she insisted. "Really. I've got my hat today."

He looked doubtful, but did not try to persuade her to remain behind. She had no doubts herself that she could manage the climb and walk. It had not been vertigo that had made her pass out yesterday morning, she felt sure, but simply the heat after running and the emotional conflict she was suffering. She was touched, however, by Mac's show of concern.

They walked for some distance up the valley to where the cliffs closed in on either side, rising sheer and gaunt into the hard blue sky. A narrow path gradually took them higher and higher from the valley floor up through a rugged outcrop of tumbled boulders that looked as though tossed there by some giant hand. It was after all quite hard going, and increasingly hot, but Laura unflaggingly kept up with the others, determined not to show any sign of weakness or to be a nuisance. Mac would be only too ready to say he had doubted that she ought to come.

Eventually they came to a wide ledge and the aboriginal guide led them through a narrow cleft in the rocks to plunge down again on the other side through a deep cool chasm, where, on one side, the cliff was wet and encrusted from water seepage.

"There's a magnificent waterfall here some wet seasons," Eric told them. "I haven't seen it, of course, but the aborigines describe it as a magnificent curtain of water. You have to view it from the top of the rocks because it becomes a boiling whirlpool in here. It's caused, they say, by a spirit that lives inside the rock, who weeps for her lost love."

Laura could well believe that the place was inhabited by spirits. There was a curious silence into which now and then seemed to intrude mysterious whisperings. It may have been only the wind singing through the apertures in the rocks, or

159

through the tops of spindly trees that grew right out of the rock near the top, reaching up to the light, but it was easy to imagine spirits instead.

At last they stood at the entrance to the cave. Even Laura had to stoop to enter. To her surprise it was not as dark inside as she had expected. There was a fissure in the roof that let a shaft of light into the cavern and illuminated it perfectly. At once she was confronted with the paintings they had come to see.

"Christmas!" breathed MacDougall. "I've never seen anything like this! And to think no one ever discovered it!"

"I know," said Eric excitedly. "I was staggered. I had no idea it would be so magnificent." He added reverently, "I felt very privileged to be the first white man to see them. This is the most important find for many years. There's a potted history of the tribe here. Some of these paintings may be thousands of years old. Charlie told me that for many years not even the aborigines knew the cave existed. It had somehow been forgotten when the tribe fragmented and the old men died. Then, quite by accident, one of them, chasing a rock wallaby, discovered it again and realized what some of the stories that had puzzled them meant at last."

"How did they paint the pictures?" asked Laura, fascinated as she bent to examine details. "What do all these symbols mean?"

Eric said, "They used earth colors, and charcoal, and vegetable coloring. You'll notice it's mainly reds, yellows, ochers—all from pigments easily obtainable hereabouts. I don't know the meaning of all the symbols, and some even the aborigines don't know, but we're slowly piecing things together. I still have to come back and photograph it all, but the site must remain a secret. If tourists—or even interested scientists for that matter—start milling around, it'll deteriorate in no time. Anyway, the tribe only showed me because I gave my solemn oath not to reveal its whereabouts and they trust me." He added proudly, "I'm a blood brother."

"But I'm not," said Laura, feeling she had been greatly honored to be trusted, too, even if only for the reason MacDougall had stated—her ignorance of where they were.

"They trust Mac," Eric said, as though that was enough.

"It's very well preserved," observed MacDougall, peering closely at the walls, of which practically every square inch was decorated with paintings that were as fresh as they must have been the day they were executed.

"One of those marvelous freaks of nature," said Eric. "It has been little disturbed, of course, but also because of the peculiar dryness of the cave, remarkable when you think of the seepage in the chasm we just came through. The conditions are absolutely perfect."

Laura could see that even though he had seen the paintings previously, he was in a great state of excitement. They lingered for some time while Eric made some more notes, and then presently made their way out of the cave, through the waterfall chasm, and started down the long winding path to the valley floor.

Laura, pausing behind the others to look down from the top, realized that they had climbed much higher than it had seemed on the way up. A way down the winding valley she could see the glimmer of the water hole where she had been swimming that morning near the camp. And from her vantage point the ranges stretched interminably into the distance, wild and rugged and possessed of a savage beauty.

"Come on, Laura. . . ." MacDougall looked back, calling impatiently.

Laura descended reluctantly and caught up. MacDougall made her walk ahead of him. They had scarcely gone any distance when the accident happened. Eric, who was just ahead of Laura, turned and called, "Not going too fast for you, Laura?"

"No," she replied.

As he turned back, he caught his foot against a stone, stumbled, grabbed at the rock face, but could not find anything to grasp there, and was thrown even more off balance. The next moment Laura was gasping in horror as her brother plunged over the edge of the path.

Laura screamed, "Eric!" She ran to the spot and MacDougall, who was a few paces behind, raced to her side. Charlie, who was some distance ahead of them, ran back.

"Eric . . ." Laura looked down in fear and dismay at his still, crumpled form, not far below them, but precariously supported by a thin sapling ghost gum growing out of the cliff. It had miraculously prevented him from falling farther, but it looked as though it might snap off or be wrenched from its footing at any second. She was sure Eric was dead, he lay so still. Impulsively, she made a move to scramble down to him, but MacDougall's strong fingers gripped her arm and roughly dragged her back.

"Stay here," he commanded. "We don't want you going over too."

She watched fearfully as MacDougall and Charlie carefully slid down the slope, which offered only clumps of grass as foot- and hand-holds. When Eric suddenly moved, her relief was momentarily obliterated by the fear that he would not realize how precarious his position was, and either fall farther or inadvertently cause the sapling to snap off. She closed her eyes after glancing to the bottom of the cliff, a hundred feet below.

"Don't move, Eric!" she cried in panic, but MacDougall and Charlie had already reached him.

Laura heard her brother say in a surprised sort of voice, "Damn silly thing to do. I'm afraid I've broken my leg."

MacDougall bent over him. Laura felt the seconds drag like years. Finally, she heard MacDougall say, "We'll have to get you back to the path, Prof. It's too dangerous to leave you here until we can get help. This sapling won't hold your weight much longer. Do you think you can make it? We'll bring a stretcher up to get you out from there."

"Whatever you say, Mac," said Eric. Laura could hear the pain in his voice, but there was determination, too.

She wished she could help, but knew that she would only be a hindrance, so she could only stand and pray as Charlie aided Eric onto MacDougall's back and steadied them both during the slow perilous climb back to the path. It was not far but one false step could have meant disaster for all three. Laura's heart was in her mouth. Half a dozen times, as MacDougall struggled to keep a foothold on the stony slope, she saw them

162

all hurtling down into the valley, and a feeling of utter desolation washed over her.

But her worst fears were not realized. After what seemed an age, but was only a few minutes, MacDougall climbed onto the path with his burden. Laura assisted Charlie to lift Eric off his back and make him as comfortable as possible on the ground. The professor did not complain, but she could see by his contorted face that the perilous trip back up the cliff face had caused him great pain. He looked at her and smiled, and then promptly passed out.

MacDougall said, "You'll have to stay with him, Laura. We'll be back as quickly as we can. Will you be all right?"

"Of course I will!" Did he have to look at her as though he expected her to pass out too? She watched them go, then sat near her brother, trying not to worry. MacDougall had assured her that Eric was all right. It was just the pain that had made him pass out. She fervently hoped he had no worse injuries than a broken leg. He had not fallen far, and he had rolled most of the way, breaking his leg only because it had twisted under him as he came in contact with the tree.

While she waited, the bush seemed unnaturally quiet, until a pied butcher-bird suddenly appeared and perched on a nearby sapling, warbling tunefully. Laura, however, was unmoved by its vibrant music today. She was too worried about Eric.

After what seemed an interminable wait, Laura glimpsed the rescue party heading toward the cliff. A few moments later, Eric stirred and regained consciousness. He looked at Laura with an apologetic grin.

"Never had an accident in the field before. Always too damned careful. Stupid thing to do. . . ."

"It could happen to anyone," Laura said, and because she felt MacDougall was bound to blame her, she added, "It was having me along. You were too anxious to see that I was all right."

"Rubbish," he retorted, giving a wince of pain as he moved slightly. "It wasn't your fault! It was my own stupidity."

The rescue party appeared on the path just ahead, and

Laura had never felt more thankful to see anyone. A team of eager bearers were carrying a makeshift stretcher made from a piece of tarpaulin lashed between two straight saplings. They laid Eric on it and slowly the procession set off down the narrow path.

"What are we going to do?" Laura asked, walking behind with MacDougall.

"Splint up the leg and take him to Ulurkura Station. I'll try and call up the Flying Doctor from here on the truck radio, and they'll send a plane to meet us there. They'll take him to the hospital in Alice Springs."

"Is that far?" Laura asked. "The station, I mean." She was thinking of Eric in MacDougall's truck, jolted about, in agony.

"Far enough," said MacDougall, with a grim expression. "But if we set off as soon as we can, we might make it before nightfall."

MacDougall did not waste a moment once they reached the camp. He went immediately to radio the Flying Doctor, while Laura gave Eric aspirins to ease the pain, and then assisted him to drink the hot sweet tea one of the aboriginal women brought to her. Everyone stood around rather helplessly, their usually happy faces showing deep concern.

MacDougall was smiling when he came back to them. "Got through easily, thank goodness. The plane will be there before we are. They'll alert the Mortons. Now, let's see about a temporary splint for this leg of yours, Prof."

"Glad you decided to stick around today," murmured Eric gratefully, adding with wry humor, "It would have been a bit of a hike on one leg otherwise."

MacDougall glanced briefly at Laura. "I daresay it wouldn't have happened at all if we hadn't been here."

She flinched. He meant her, of course. He was blaming her as she had thought he would.

MacDougall said, "We'd better clear a space in the back of the truck, Laura, down the middle."

"I'll do it." Laura was glad to be able to make herself useful, so while MacDougall splinted Eric's leg, she arranged the remaining gear in the back of the truck so that the stretcher could be wedged in securely.

Their departure was abrupt and hurried. As soon as everything was ready, MacDougall was impatient to leave. Laura stayed in the back of the truck with her brother, and a little sadly waved good-bye to the friendly waving people they were leaving behind.

MacDougall drove with infinite care to avoid jolting the patient more than necessary, but nevertheless the first hour of the journey was, Laura could tell from his face, very uncomfortable for Eric, although he did not once complain or groan. Instead, he made a joke of the whole thing and upbraided Laura for looking so solemn.

MacDougall halted once or twice to check that everything was all right in the back. Once, sensing her tension, he patted Laura's shoulder and said, "He'll be all right, don't worry." His touch and his kindly tone were almost more than she could bear.

Eventually, they came to a graded dirt path, which, although unsealed, and very uneven, was infinitely superior to the rough bush paths they had traveled on out of the valley. The sun was setting when the truck halted once more. Laura thought it was just MacDougall coming to check on them yet again, but when his face appeared at the opening in the tarpaulin, he said, "Okay, we've arrived."

Laura breathed a deep sigh of relief, and Eric muttered a thankful, "Pheeww!"

Laura jumped down from the truck. She could see no homestead, nothing to indicate that this was a cattle station, nothing but dust and a few straggly trees and clumps of spinifex and other grasses.

Then she turned and saw the small white plane standing on what must have been a landing strip. On its dusty fuselage was the insignia of the Royal Flying Doctor Service. And beyond, she now saw in the distance a cluster of buildings with a long straight road leading to them. There was a cloud of dust approaching along the road.

Two men carrying a stretcher were coming toward them, followed by a girl in nurse's uniform.

"G'day, Mac," one of the men greeted MacDougall briefly.

They wasted no time, but moved quickly to the back of the truck to take charge of Eric. The nurse shot Laura a friendly, sympathetic smile. Laura stood a little apart and watched as they carefully transferred Eric into the aircraft. As they were doing this the approaching cloud of dust became a truck, which skidded to a halt near MacDougall's and a man got out. He shook hands with MacDougall, who introduced him to Laura as Jack Morton from Ulurkura Station.

Then he said to her reassuringly, "Eric'll be in the hospital in the Alice very soon."

"Yes," she answered. She glanced at him. This was the MacDougall she wished existed all the time. An outrageous thought rushed through her mind. Perhaps during the next few days, alone with him, she would find a way to break down the barrier he had erected. Perhaps she could, by showing her love, banish the bitter, contemptuous MacDougall and resurrect the tender loving man she felt sure he really was. She would convince him that if he would let her love him, she would never leave him—as Valerie had.

His voice broke into her crazy thoughts. "If they've got room, you might as well go with them. It'll save you a good deal of discomfort on the return trip, and anyway, you ought to be with your brother."

Laura opened her mouth to object. She felt as though he had punched her in the stomach, and her knees were crumpling under her. The rosy dream she had so foolishly let distract her dispersed into a million fragments. He was not going to give her the chance to try to make it come true.

"But I . . ." she started to say, not knowing what she really wanted to say. Not her thoughts of a moment ago, certainly. She protested feebly, "But my luggage is at Camel Creek."

"You seem to have managed without it quite well during the past few days," he pointed out dryly. "You can collect it later, or have it sent on." He added pointedly, "I would have thought after all your effort to see him, you would want to be with your brother."

She did. She wanted to stay with Eric, but she also wanted to be with this hard, aggressive man, even though he obviously did not want her. He was glad of this opportunity to be rid of her for the remainder of the trip. There was nothing she could say. The doctor came over to them, and MacDougall immediately asked if Laura could go on the plane with them.

"Sure . . . no worries," said the young sandy-haired doctor readily. "Plenty of room." He added, "Lucky for the Prof you were on the spot, Mac. It's a bad break." He turned quickly to Laura. "But nothing to worry about, Miss Fairchild."

MacDougall said, "Well, I won't hold you up." He turned to Laura. His expression was inscrutable as he drawled, "Nice meeting you, Laura. I hope all goes well for you. Good-bye."

There was no regret in his voice. He didn't even smile. He just turned away to speak to Jack Morton, who was asking if he wanted to stay the night at the station. Laura, with a tight feeling around her heart heard him say, yes, he'd be glad to, and enjoy a decent meal for a change. Hot tears blinding her eyes, she ran to the aircraft and scrambled aboard.

A few moments later the little plane was speeding along the dusty runway. Laura waved to the two men standing at the edge of it near the trucks. MacDougall was still unsmiling as he raised his arm briefly in a salute. The plane rose and circled several hundred feet above the ground. By then all Laura could see in the dying glow from the sun were two clouds of dust on the long straight road as MacDougall and Jack Morton drove toward the homestead. The ache in her heart was as real as Eric's broken leg.

"Nice meeting you," MacDougall had said. But he had not meant it. He was glad to be rid of her.

Chapter Twelve

It seemed to Laura as she stepped out of the shower into her motel room that the past few days must have been a dream—or a nightmare. Had she really stowed away on a truck and traveled for days with a big taciturn man with dark blond hair, steely gray eyes and a bitter twist to his mouth? A man who could feel tenderness and passion, and yet who saw both as weakness; a man who had never missed an opportunity to cut her down to size? Had MacDougall even existed?

"Robert MacDougall." She said his name softly, with a little sigh, and smiled wryly at her thoughts as she hooked up the new bra she had bought and remembered the one Caesar had chewed up. That had been real enough, as had her embarrassment and Mac's ribald laughter.

She pulled on the new pale-gray slacks and hibiscus-pink shirt she had purchased yesterday, and regarded her reflection in the mirror with satisfaction. This morning, still clad in her scruffy and dirty gear, she had left the motel early, and had sallied forth into Alice Springs to buy some new clothes. She had felt sure people were staring at her disheveled appearance, but it is doubtful if anyone noticed the slim shapely girl with the gamin hairstyle, unless it was to remark on her startlingly attractive but sad eyes, contrasting with the vivaciousness of her whole expression, which even worry, tiredness and heartache could not entirely dispel.

The night before the girl at the reception desk in the motel had looked at her dubiously when she had asked for a room and had seemed suspicious of the fact that she had no luggage. Even the story of her brother's accident had sounded bizarre, related in the slick modern reception area of the motel. However, the girl had reluctantly given her a room in the end since she had been able to pay for it in advance.

Eric, she had been told, would be in hospital for several weeks. He would then need to convalesce for some time before he would regain the full use of his leg. Laura sighed for him as she outlined her lips with the new pink lipstick she had bought, but not bothering with any other makeup. He was bound to be very angry with himself about the whole unfortunate business.

She hurried off to the hospital that afternoon just as soon as she knew she would be able to visit him, anxious to see how he was. He was delighted to see her, and as concerned about her as she was about him.

"There's no need for you to hang around here," he said straight away. "You might as well go down to Sydney. I can write that note to Elsie Lindsay right now."

"Don't be silly!" she exclaimed. "I'm not going to leave you."

"Now, Laura," he said firmly. "I don't want you to feel you've got to . . ."

She raised a hand to stop him. "Eric . . . it's no use your arguing. I'm staying until you're out of hospital. It's a chance for us to see something of each other after all. There's no point in my being in Sydney and you here."

"No, I suppose not." He looked thoughtful for a moment, then continued, "I'm going to have to convalesce for quite a while after I get out of here. It'll be ages before I can complete my work in the valley."

"I know . . . I'm sorry. It was rotten luck," Laura said sympathetically.

"I suppose the sensible thing to do would be to go down to Sydney as soon as I can leave the hospital," Eric said.

Laura smiled. "That's what I was thinking. And if it's too much for your Mrs. Lindsay, we'll get a flat and I'll look after you."

He grinned at her. "Seems you turned up at an opportune moment!"

"I'm very glad I did."

"Oh, this damned leg!" he exclaimed. "Why did it have to happen right now? It'll drive me crazy being out of action for weeks."

Laura had fully expected this kind of reaction. She said, "Can't you be doing something with your notes? There seemed to be a lot of notebooks in that satchel we brought back."

He brightened a little. "Yes, I suppose I could make a start, sorting them out and correlating information. . . . Yes, I might as well get on with it. It's all going into a book eventually."

Laura said, "If you want anything typed, I expect I could hire a typewriter from somewhere."

He looked surprised. "You can type?"

"Yes. Quite fast too."

He regarded her thoughtfully for a moment, then said, "Well, that puts a whole new complexion on things. There are a couple of papers I want to submit to scientific journals, so I could get cracking on those right away if you can type them for me." He paused, frowning, then added, "There's just one thing. . . ."

"What's that?"

"All my early field notes, the bulk of the whole project really, are back at Camel Creek. I used to bundle them up and send them in with Mac each trip, to save carting too much around with me. It's all in safekeeping at the hotel. Mrs. Burdekin was looking after a few of my other belongings too."

"My luggage is still down there too," said Laura. "I was

thinking of phoning through and asking Mrs. Burdekin to send it up on the next bus. She could send yours too."

"That's a good idea," agreed Eric, then after a moment's consideration, he changed his mind. "I wonder, Laura . . . if it wouldn't be too much trouble for you to go down and collect it all personally. I know I'm being fussy, but I should hate to lose any of my notes, and things can go astray. I should feel a lot happier if you would go and bring it all back yourself. Would you mind very much? I think there's a bus on Wednesday from here, and one back on Friday, but you'd better check."

Laura said, "Of course it won't be any trouble. I'd like to see Mrs. Burdekin and apologize for causing them worry, in any case. I'll check on the bus as soon as I leave here."

"Mac will be back," said Eric casually. "You could let him know how things are."

"Yes, I'll do that," Laura said without a quaver.

Eric gave her a quizzical smile. "I reckon he'll be glad to see you again."

Laura sighed. "Eric, you're barking up the wrong tree. I told you, Mac thinks I'm a frivolous irresponsible child, and I've given him plenty of reason for his opinion."

"Have you? I got the impresson he admired you tremendously," Eric said. "I think you've got a bit of a chip on your shoulder, Laura. Anyway, let him know what's happening, will you?"

She agreed that she would, and so when the next bus went through Laura was on it, bound for Camel Creek once more. Traveling from the opposite direction, the bus arrived in Camel Creek around midday. As before, the long detour from the highway was made for Laura's benefit alone, there being no other passengers for the remote settlement.

She alighted with a curious feeling of familiarity and pleasure. The cluster of heat-shimmering buildings in the featureless landscape was hardly beautiful, or even picturesque. In fact it was quite ugly, but the past days had given her an affinity with it all she had never expected to find. She would always remember it of course as the place where she fell in love, she thought with sudden painful sentimentality.

Drowsing in the midday sun, its dusty main street deserted, Camel Creek looked like some abandoned film set. There was no one to board the bus, no parcels to deliver or pick up, and the driver paused only briefly to set Laura down, then disappeared in a cloud of dust. When the dust had settled, it was as though there had been no disturbance.

As Laura walked toward the hotel, a man came out of the milk bar opposite, a tall broad-shouldered man in khaki shirt and trousers, and wearing a battered wide-brimmed hat. Her heart turned over. Instinctively she rushed forward, his name on her lips, but when he turned, she saw with a surge of disappointment that it was not MacDougall. Her heart plummeted, and she walked disconsolately on toward the hotel.

Mrs. Burdekin was delighted to see her and not in the slightest reproachful because Laura had disappeared that afternoon just over a week ago. It seemed now to Laura so much longer.

"I've put you back in the same room," the hotel proprietress said.

"Thank you for all your trouble, Mrs. Burdekin," said Laura sincerely.

"Why don't you slip into the dining room now and have some lunch," suggested Mrs. Burdekin kindly. "We can have another chat presently."

Laura hesitated, then ventured casually, "Is Mr. Mac-Dougall back yet?"

Mrs. Burdekin nodded, giving Laura a mildly inquisitive look. She was obviously very intrigued by the whole business of Laura going with MacDougall. She said, "He got back yesterday."

Laura's heart immediately leaped treacherously. He might be here—even in the dining room at this very minute.

But Mrs. Burdekin disappointed her again. "He went straight home to Nilla Nilla." She treated Laura to another searching look. "I daresay he won't be back in town for at least a week."

"He will be anxious to know how my brother is," Laura said, swallowing her disappointment. "Perhaps I could telephone him?"

172

"Of course," agreed Mrs. Burdekin. "You just let me know when you want the call put through."

"I'll do it straight after lunch," Laura decided.

She escaped into the dining room and was thankful to find only two other people there. The two men were engrossed in earnest conversation and did not spare her more than a cursory glance as she walked in. She learned from Mavis the waitress that they were tourists passing through.

There were no phones in the hotel rooms, so Laura was obliged to use the one in the little office behind the reception desk, to which Mrs. Burdekin led her as soon as she said she was ready to make the call. Laura felt nervous. She longed to hear his voice and yet in a way wished she did not have to speak to him.

Mrs. Burdekin rang the exchange and gave the number. She handed the receiver to Laura. "It's ringing. . . ." She then slipped out and discreetly closed the door.

Laura held the receiver in nervous fingers, moistening her dry lips with her tongue. The ringing went on and on until she felt certain no one was going to answer it. This gave her mingled feelings of relief and frustration. The ordeal would be postponed, but sooner or later she would have to go through with it.

Then just as she was about to replace the receiver, the ringing stopped and a male voice said crisply, "Hello!"

Laura's heart leapt but at the same instant she knew it was not MacDougall.

"Hello," she faltered. "Is Mr. MacDougall there?"

"No. Sorry, he isn't. He'll be back later. This is Carslake. Is there a message?"

Laura decided she would leave a message. There was no point in talking directly to Mac; it would only be a painful experience.

She said, "Yes, please. Would you tell him Laura Fairchild rang to let him know that Eric is all right, and that we'll both be going down to Sydney as soon as they let him out of hospital."

"Okay," said the man, who Laura supposed must be MacDougall's manager. "He'll be glad to hear it. Bad business, but not so bad as it might have been. Righto, I'll tell him. The professor will be in touch himself in due course, I expect."

"Yes, he will," said Laura. "Thank you very much, Mr. Carslake."

There must have been a slight hesitation in her voice because he said, "Anything else?"

"No . . . that's all . . ." Laura said slowly. What else could she say? What message could she leave for MacDougall other than that? Then hastily she added, "Just say thanks for everything."

"Sure thing," promised the manager. "All the best then. Cheerio."

"Cheerio . . ." Laura heard the click at the other end and slowly replaced the receiver with an empty feeling inside her.

She went straight up to her room and lay down on the bed, staring at the pink shaded light and the fan whirling in the middle of the ceiling, and listening to a fly beating itself against the window, too apathetic even to get up and let it out or swat it. Room 13, she mused wryly. She might have believed it was unlucky except that she wasn't superstitious.

She was a fool, though, she told herself over and over. It was just as well MacDougall was not in town, and had not even answered the telephone. She would be in a worse emotional state than ever. There was no sense in dwelling on it. She must put him right out of her mind and heart and get on with living. There was plenty to do, plenty to think about, with Eric being in the hospital and wanting to work on his notes. Helping him would take her mind off herself, and once they were down in Sydney, she would be able to make plans. . . .

She sighed. It should be exciting, looking forward to this new life she was going to make for herself, but all she felt was a dreary acceptance of a gray future that without MacDougall seemed meaningless. Perhaps, she thought bleakly, she would be like the man she loved, carrying forever in her heart the memory of a love that would not die.

She stayed in her room for most of the afternoon. There was little else to do anyway, except sit in the lounge, and there someone might talk to her, which at the moment was the last thing she wanted. An hour before dinner she showered and changed into one of the summer dresses in her suitcase. It was a simple shift in pale avocado green cotton, and looked as well as felt cool.

She sat at the dressing table looking at herself in the mirror for some moments in a detached kind of way. She looked no different, she thought, except for lack of makeup, at least no different on the outside, but inside there was a whole world of difference, a new person in fact. She smiled wryly at her reflection and opened her makeup case, staring for a moment at its contents, and then she closed it, allowing herself only a light touch of lipstick. She might use it again, she thought, but just now even the sight of it reminded her too poignantly of MacDougall.

She felt restless, so decided to go for a walk around the town as it was cooler now. There was not much to see in the town, so she strolled toward a patch of trees on the perimeter that bravely declared itself to be a park. There was a notice board with Camel Creek Park painted on it and a brief inscription commemorating the local notable who had established it. There was no lawn beneath the gums, pepper trees and she-oaks, but two or three rickety wooden seats were scattered about amid the thick carpeting of brown leaves.

A flock of pink and gray galahs suddenly wheeled in the sky and settled into the trees. Laura walked into the park to look at them more closely, and at the same time a cloud of dust on the road approaching from the west caught her eye. She paused to watch the vehicle that was speeding along the dirt road. As it flashed past on its way into town she knew a sudden lurching of her heart. Surely that was MacDougall's truck, and the driver, with his hat pushed back . . .

"Oh, don't be ridiculous!" she told herself, turning away and striding purposefully toward the tree where the parrots were chattering loudly. Mrs. Burdekin had said he wouldn't be back for a week. There were dozens of trucks like his and practically every man in the Outback wore a similar kind of hat.

She stared up into the trees, determined to concentrate her

attention on the birds, but the sight of their vivid pink and gray plumage only reminded her of the first time a flock had risen from the road in front of the truck one morning and Mac had told her what they were. Mac . . . MacDougall . . . Robert . . . She sighed. Everything was an evocative reminder of the man.

The parrots, muttering among themselves as they clawed their way among the leaves, nibbling at blossoms and seeds, every now and then paused in their waddling gait to look down at her with saucy eyes, and eventually she burst out laughing, although cheerful was hardly the way she felt.

"Laura . . ." His hand on her shoulder startled her as much as his voice, and, shaken to the core, she turned incredulously.

"Mac . . . !" Looking at him, tall, brown, wearing the familiar khaki shirt and trousers, his hat pushed back on his head, she thought she must be dreaming. But he was real, as the firm feel of his fingers through her thin cotton dress confirmed. So it must have been his truck she had seen. Either he had seen her as he passed or Mrs. Burdekin had told him where she had gone. She had been careful to tell her this time that she was just going for a walk around the town.

"What are you doing back here?" she asked, so happy to see him.

"Bob Carslake told me you'd phoned." He took his hand away.

"Yes, I did . . . I left a message for you."

He nodded. "But you didn't say you were at Camel Creek. I thought you'd rung from the Alice. So I phoned the hospital and they let me speak to Eric. He told me you'd come down to collect your luggage, and his gear." There was an odd expression in his gray eyes, almost as though he was as nervous in her company as she was in his.

"Mrs. Burdekin said you wouldn't be back in Camel Creek for a week or more," Laura said, wondering why he was there now.

"I didn't intend to be. But when Eric told me you were down here, well, I thought I might as well drive in and say hello."

She looked at him, puzzled. "It was a long way to come just to . . . say hello." She was at a loss. She would never have expected him to do a thing like that. Surely that day he had seen her off on the plane with Eric he had been relieved that he would not have to see her again. She remembered his face then—hard, cold, totally indifferent to her.

His gaze was searching. "Perhaps we have more to say to each other than just hello."

She shrugged. "I suppose Eric told you more about what he intends to do?"

He thrust his hands into his pockets. "Yes. I talked him out of it."

Laura's mouth dropped open in astonishment. "You what?"

"I talked him out of it. I have a much better idea."

There was a glimmer of a smile playing about his lips now, but she noticed that there was also a nerve twitching at the corner of his mouth, in him a sign of stress. She felt annoyed with him. What right had he to persuade Eric to change his plans, without even consulting her?

"I wish you'd tell me about it," she said a trifle acidly.

"Come and sit down for a few minutes and I will," he said. He put a hand under her elbow and guided her to one of the park seats. His touch, she realized with dismay, still had the power to bring fire into her veins as fiercely as ever. They sat down, and Laura deliberately placed herself as far from him as she could. He took off his hat and laid it on the seat, raking his fingers through his flattened hair and looking at her intently with, she thought, some apprehension before he spoke again.

"Well," she said abruptly. "Go on. . . ."

"I suggested to Eric," MacDougall said slowly, "that he might prefer to spend his convalescence at Nilla Nilla."

"Your place!" Laura was dumbfounded.

He nodded. "He can write his notes up just as planned, and you can help him. We've got a pretty good typewriter, and Mrs. Carslake is an ex-nurse, so he'll be in good hands. He agreed it would be better than foisting himself on this Mrs. Lindsay he stays with in Sydney, or expecting you to look after him as well as help with his work. He'll be on the spot too, to check points with members of the tribe he's been living with, and of course once the leg is okay he can go straight off and finish the job of notating those cave paintings." He was watching closely for her reaction, and Laura bit her lip. Living at MacDougall's place was the last thing she could have envisaged, and she was not sure she liked the idea at all. She took a deep breath.

"He doesn't really want to go to Sydney, does he?"

Mac smiled. "Right! Your brother, Laura, is not a city man. He only goes when he has to, and because he needs a base somewhere. He said it was up to you, though, that if you'd rather go to Sydney . . ."

She hesitated only a moment. She could not oppose the idea. She had made up her mind she would not be a burden to Eric in any way, and the very least she could do for him was to type his articles and notes. Perhaps it wouldn't be so bad. MacDougall would probably not be around all that much. She glanced at him. No doubt he thought she was anxious to get back to the city.

She said, "I'm happy to do what Eric wants."

MacDougall smiled. "Living on a cattle station will be yet another new experience for you!" He was only faintly mocking.

"It's very generous of you, Mac," she said. "I'm sure Eric is very grateful. I . . . I am too. Thank you."

He shrugged and regarded her quizzically for a moment before he said, "There's just one thing."

"What's that?"

"Something we have to straighten out, Laura."

She was startled. "Straighten out? What do you mean?" It sounded ominous.

"Between you and me."

She said slowly, "Is there anything to straighten out? I thought—" The intensity of his gaze stopped her.

"Eric told me how you feel about me," he said.

Laura closed her eyes, a wave of humiliation washing over her. *Oh, why did Eric have to interfere?* So now Mac was going to tell her what a fool she was, and impress on her that just because he had invited her and her brother to stay a while at Nilla Nilla it didn't mean anything, and she'd better not get any ideas about him.

She jumped up and ran a few steps, burning with shame and anger at Eric for betraying her confidence. It would be unbearable, she realized, to fall in with their plans now that MacDougall knew the truth, but what alternative did she have?

She turned around just as he came up to her. "Look . . ." she said jerkily, "Eric got it all wrong. Surely you realize that." She managed a short laugh. "Really! He doesn't know anything about it . . . about us . . . he was just teasing, being romantic or something. I mean, you would never have got such a crazy idea yourself, would you?"

"No," he answered slowly, "although there were times when . . ."

"Yes, well, two people thrown together like that . . . th . . . things were bound to happen. We're only human after all, but you made it quite clear . . . and anyway I thought you realized so far as I was concerned . . ."

"You did spell out your feelings that last morning," he agreed dryly, "before you ran off into the bush. I must say you were pretty convincing. You left me in no doubt what you thought of me. . . ."

"Well, I was a bit . . . well, I overdid it a bit," she confessed. "I don't really think you're exactly despicable. . . ." She paused, then firmly added, "There's nothing to straighten out, Mac. You needn't be afraid I'll be mooning around after you if we come to Nilla Nilla for Eric's convalescence. I wouldn't dream of embarrassing you in that way, anyway. I don't really think we need to talk about it anymore. Can't we just forget all that and be friends?"

His mouth twisted ironically. He grasped her arms and looked fiercely into her wavering green eyes. "Laura, you are a terrible liar! I told you that once before. So, let's stop this playacting and tell the truth."

She struggled to free herself but he held her fast. "I've told you the truth," she persisted, and then angrily threw at him, "Stop trying to pretend otherwise, or can't you bear it if every woman you set eyes on doesn't fall at your feet? Can't you bear it that I am indifferent to you? Is it such a blow to your vanity?"

He did not answer, but pulled her against him hard and smiled infuriatingly down at her, his mouth hovering inches from her own.

"Let go of me!" she cried, through clenched teeth. "I don't know what you're trying to prove, but it won't change anything. I hate you! Do you hear, I hate you! You're a brute!"

He said softly, "If only you knew how desirable you are like this—when your eyes are flashing anger, and your mouth is saying things you know perfectly well you don't mean."

"Ohhh!" She felt she was going to explode. But there was no fight left in her. She was helpless in his grasp, and when he took advantage of her sudden lack of resistance and bent his head to cover her mouth with his, tantalizingly tender at first deliberately to arouse her, then with a mounting passion that surpassed even the night of the storm, she was beyond all opposition and yielded to him in spite of herself.

As his lips moved on hers, hungrily probing, and his hands held her imprisoned with their urgent caressing, every nerve in her body tingled, every fiber in her being responded to him as though she had no will, and she relaxed against him, gradually bending to his will, drowning in the brief stolen joy and not even caring that her very submission told him what he suspected, and for some reason needed to prove yet again. So, what did it matter now? If humiliating her gratified him, then let it be so. She could pretend no longer.

At last he lifted his head and his eyes were triumphant. "You don't kiss me as though you hate me," he said huskily.

He pressed her head against his chest and slid his fingers through her hair, stroking the nape of her neck, setting her nerves on fire anew, and she was incapable of preventing the torment he was inflicting on her because of the sweet rapture of being in his arms, whatever the reason.

"Or is that the way you always kiss a man?" he persisted.

"Maybe . . ." she said defensively, reluctantly returning to reality.

He stiffened slightly. "Laura . . ."

She raised her eyes and looked at him coolly. "You formed an opinion of me that first night, so why change it?"

"Because . . ." He seemed reluctant to go on, and she felt there was some inner conflict behind the steady scrutiny of his gray eyes, and the nerve in his cheek was twitching again. He said, "I behaved that night, and later, in a way perhaps I should not have done. I did rather take advantage . . . of our situation."

She breathed in sharply. "There's no need to apologize. There were extenuating circumstances." She smiled, carefully controlling her face muscles so he would not guess what anguish he was causing her, and added lightly, "Look, just let's say we've both quite enjoyed the encounters. Nothing wrong with that, is there? Let's leave it at that. None of it meant any more to me than it did to you." She paused and felt now that she must tell him. "Mac . . . I know about Valerie. You talked about her when you were delirious, and later Eric told me the story. I'm so sorry . . . and I understand how you feel."

His eyes had narrowed slightly at the mention of his wife's name, and now held hers with a new intensity.

"It must have been terrible for you," she said, "but I know what it's like to love someone and lose them. . . ."

"Do you? Was there someone . . . back in England?" His tone was sharply inquiring.

She glanced away, wishing she had not said that. "I don't want to talk about it," she said, "any more than you do. I don't know why we're standing here talking like this anyhow. Let's go back to the hotel. Are you staying the night? You won't drive back in the dark will you?"

"No . . ." He did not move. "Laura . . . the night I was ill, you said something . . . but afterward when you blew up . . . I thought I must have been mistaken, and it was just a dream. That night is still hazy. . . ." He paused. "But when Eric said—"

"It *was* a dream!" she broke in sharply, and then angrily

said, "Do you have to do this? Do you have to go on tormenting me just because you want to prove your masculinity, your infallible magnetism?"

"No," he said, "I'm still just afraid to believe . . . in what I want to believe in. I'm still afraid that in my clumsy way I may have caused you to have feelings that were no more than a spontaneous reaction to a highly charged moment. . . ."

Laura stared at him, uncomprehending. "I don't know what you're talking about," she murmured, utterly perplexed.

He sighed. "No. Because I'm as reluctant to commit myself as you are." He lifted a strand of her hair and smoothed it into her head. "Laura, I tried fighting it too . . . all the way back in the truck I was still trying, but two whole days without you was hell."

Laura's eyes widened incredulously. "You can't mean that! You were glad to be rid of me earlier than you expected."

"In a way, yes. I thought I could put you out of my mind, that it was all just a physical thing, but I couldn't, and when Eric said he thought . . . well, he was sure you were in love with me . . . I didn't dare believe him. But I had to see you to find out." He paused and looked a trifle sheepish. "Well, now you know. . . ."

"I'm not sure that I do," Laura breathed softly. "I thought you despised me . . . you treated me like a spoiled child . . . you derided me. . . ."

"Because you were getting under my skin in spite of myself, you witch!" he said. "I had to keep telling myself that you weren't suitable . . . that you'd never stick . . . oh, Laura, I couldn't bear the possibility of being disappointed a second time, to find it was all an illusion."

"Because of Valerie?"

He nodded. "My common sense told me you would be another Valerie. And that was a ghastly mistake. When we parted the first time, it should have been final. I don't know what madness made us marry. Some sort of crazy belief that Fate had engineered our meeting again, I suppose, that the film company wanting to shoot a film in Australia was part of some cosmic purpose for us. It wasn't. Her career was getting nowhere, despite the film, and I was lonely . . . those were the real reasons . . . but there's no point in going over it. . . ."

"But you still love her," Laura said soberly. "When you were delirious, you cried out to her not to leave you. . . ."

He looked at her sadly. "Did I? I suppose I might have done so, but not because I still love her, Laura. Oh, yes, I begged her not to go that night . . . out of pride more than love, an unwillingness to admit defeat, and besides she was taking my child. . . ."

"That must have been terrible. . . ." Laura murmured, filled with compassion for him.

"After she and the child were drowned," he went on, "I wrapped myself in a cocoon of self-pity and remorse. I kidded myself it had been a happy marriage, that we had loved each other. And I kept away from women. I never wanted to go through that kind of nightmare again. And then you had to stow away on my truck. . . ."

Laura said slowly, "I didn't want to fall in love with you. . . ."

A smile curved his lips. "But you did?"

She admitted it at last. "Yes."

He drew her closer. "Laura . . . my darling . . ."

She sighed deeply, "Oh, Mac . . ." She raised her eyes to his, and as a wave of tenderness swept over her she whispered, "Robert . . ."

He touched her lips with his. "You called me Robert that night I was delirious, didn't you?"

"Yes . . ."

"And you said you loved me?"

She flushed. "Yes." She had to tell him then how she had believed he was talking to her, and how later she had realized he was thinking not of her but of Valerie.

"I was sure it wasn't a dream," he said, smiling with satisfaction. "It was all I could remember—you saying you loved me and using my first name—and yet it seemed so improbable." He tilted her chin with a gentle fingertip and chuckled. "No wonder you were so uptight the next morning. Oh, my poor Laura, you must have felt so humiliated. If only I'd realized why you wanted to run away."

"I just wanted to run and run and never set eyes on you again."

"And I was frantic with worry when you didn't come back. I thought you'd just run off a little way until you cooled down, but when I called you and you didn't answer, I began to panic. You can't imagine how I felt, Laura, when I realized you must be lost. I knew then that I loved you, but it was too late, there was no chance you would love me, I thought. I'd made you hate me, and everything else was just wishful thinking." He kissed her again. "Have we straightened things out, do you think?"

Her eyes sparkled with happiness. "I think so . . . but we can talk about it all later if we want to." She added hesitantly, "May I call you Robert now . . . not just to myself?"

"Please . . ." He traced the planes of her face with a fingertip. "I think I can allow that special intimacy now!"

"Oh, Robert . . ." She clung to him, his heartbeat pounding against her ear, and for a moment she held her breath as though if she didn't he might somehow slip away from her and disappear. Then she whispered, "Robert . . . Robert MacDougall, I love you so much, I don't think I can bear it."

They stood silently in each other's arms for some moments as the sun blazed down over the horizon, taking another day with it and leaving the fiery red landscape to darken, and the shadows to enclose them as they stood beneath the trees, as close as if they were one.

At last MacDougall said, "Will you marry me, Laura?"

"Yes," she murmured, and felt his lips close over hers once more, bringing a sweet joy to every part of her body.

Presently they moved away, arms entwined, and started slowly back toward the hotel.

MacDougall said, "You can come back to Nilla Nilla with me in the morning."

"But I promised Eric . . ." Laura exclaimed.

"We'll drive up together," he answered, "and I'll see if I can persuade the hospital to let the Flying Doctor bring him down to Nilla Nilla fairly soon." He smiled at her fondly. "I can't wait to have you there, under my own roof, with me all the time."

"But what about the trucking business?" Laura asked.

"I know a young fellow who'd like to take it over," he said. "He knows the country almost as well as I do."

A slight feeling of apprehension made Laura say, "But the memories, won't they still haunt you if you go back to live permanently at Nilla Nilla?"

He shook his head. "Not if you are there." He stopped and held her a little away from him, and for a moment his face clouded. "Laura . . . are you sure? Are you sure you want to marry me? You scarcely know me, and I've been such a brute to you . . . and on top of all that another woman haunts my past."

The desperate anxiety in his face told her how deeply he felt for her, and she said, "I know you better than any man I've ever known, even though at first I thought I never would. As for the past, let's leave it there, where it belongs. And I know you're not really a brute. . . ." She smiled at him teasingly. "You've asked me to marry you after all!" She felt compelled to add, "Are *you* quite sure you want to marry *me?* Aren't you still afraid I might turn out to be another Valerie?"

He tangled his fingers in her hair and pressed his lips to hers. "You've already proved you're not. I don't even have to ask if you think you'll like living at Nilla Nilla, making the Outback your home, because I know you already feel you belong. You'll love it, as I do, and you won't regret loving me or this country, Laura, I promise."

". . . and the land like a woman is true. Who loves her deeply, she loves him too," murmured Laura.

"And her . . ." He smiled.

Laura drew his lips down to hers. "Yes, I shall love, and be truly loved in return."

"So shall I." MacDougall held her close. "There'll be no savage moons for us, my Laura," he whispered. "Our moons will all be golden ones, and especially made for lovers!"

Laura was so perfectly happy she could not speak. She did

not know whether to laugh or cry. MacDougall being romantic! But she knew better than to laugh, so she buried her head against him in a silent embrace. When they walked on, it was in silence, but the silence of a harmonious companionship, with no antagonism and no misunderstandings between them anymore, only a deep abiding love.

Laura sighed with utter contentment. There was no uncertainty about her future now, only years crowded with wonderful things—and her beloved MacDougall . . . her Robert.

6 brand new Silhouette Special Editions yours for 15 days–Free!

For the reader who wants more...more story...more detail and description...more realism...and more romance...in paperback originals, 1/3 longer than our regular Silhouette Romances. Love lingers longer in new Silhouette Special Editions. Love weaves an intricate, provocative path in a third more pages than you have just enjoyed. It is love as you have always wanted it to be—and more —intriguingly depicted by your favorite Silhouette authors in the inimitable Silhouette style.

15-Day Free Trial Offer

We will send you 6 new Silhouette Special Editions to keep for 15 days absolutely free! If you decide not to keep them, send them back to us, you pay nothing. But if you enjoy them as much as we think you will, keep them and pay the invoice enclosed with your trial shipment. You will then automatically become a member of the Special Edition Book Club and receive 6 more romances every month. There is no minimum number of books to buy and you can cancel at any time.

IT'S YOUR OWN SPECIAL TIME

Contemporary romances for today's women.
Each month, six very special love stories will be yours
from SILHOUETTE. Look for them wherever books are sold
or order now from the coupon below.

$1.50 each

Hampson	☐ 1 ☐ 4 ☐ 16 ☐ 27 ☐ 28 ☐ 52 ☐ 94	Browning	☐ 12 ☐ 38 ☐ 53 ☐ 73 ☐ 93
Stanford	☐ 6 ☐ 25 ☐ 35 ☐ 46 ☐ 58 ☐ 88	Michaels	☐ 15 ☐ 32 ☐ 61 ☐ 87
		John	☐ 17 ☐ 34 ☐ 57 ☐ 85
Hastings	☐ 13 ☐ 26	Beckman	☐ 8 ☐ 37 ☐ 54 ☐ 96
Vitek	☐ 33 ☐ 47 ☐ 84	Wisdom	☐ 49 ☐ 95
Wildman	☐ 29 ☐ 48	Halston	☐ 62 ☐ 83

☐ 5 Goforth
☐ 7 Lewis
☐ 9 Wilson
☐ 10 Caine
☐ 11 Vernon
☐ 14 Oliver
☐ 19 Thornton
☐ 20 Fulford
☐ 21 Richards

☐ 22 Stephens
☐ 23 Edwards
☐ 24 Healy
☐ 30 Dixon
☐ 31 Halldorson
☐ 36 McKay
☐ 39 Sinclair
☐ 43 Robb
☐ 45 Carroll

☐ 50 Scott
☐ 55 Ladame
☐ 56 Trent
☐ 59 Vernon
☐ 60 Hill
☐ 63 Brent
☐ 71 Ripy
☐ 76 Hardy
☐ 78 Oliver

☐ 81 Roberts
☐ 82 Dailey
☐ 86 Adams
☐ 89 James
☐ 90 Major
☐ 92 McKay
☐ 97 Clay
☐ 98 St. George
☐ 99 Camp

$1.75 each

Stanford	☐ 100 ☐ 112 ☐ 131	Browning	☐ 113 ☐ 142 ☐ 164 ☐ 172
Hardy	☐ 101 ☐ 130 ☐ 184	Michaels	☐ 114 ☐ 146
Cork	☐ 103 ☐ 148 ☐ 188	Beckman	☐ 124 ☐ 154 ☐ 179
Vitek	☐ 104 ☐ 139 ☐ 157 ☐ 176	Roberts	☐ 127 ☐ 143 ☐ 163 ☐ 180
Dailey	☐ 106 ☐ 118 ☐ 153 ☐ 177	Trent	☐ 110 ☐ 161
Bright	☐ 107 ☐ 125	Wisdom	☐ 132 ☐ 166
Hampson	☐ 108 ☐ 119 ☐ 128 ☐ 136 ☐ 147 ☐ 151 ☐ 155 ☐ 160 ☐ 178 ☐ 185	Hunter	☐ 137 ☐ 167
		Scott	☐ 117 ☐ 169 ☐ 187
		Sinclair	☐ 123 ☐ 174

Silhouette Romance

Coming next month from
Silhouette Romances

Dreamtime by Anne Hampson

When Jane left America for the Australian Outback she had high hopes for a happy new life. But there she met domineering Scott Farnham and found herself in a heartbreaking trap.

A Secret Valentine by Dixie Browning

Now that Grace Spencer's life was finally well-ordered and sensible, she didn't need construction worker Quinn Donovan breaking down old walls and building up new expectations in her heart!

Midnight Sun by Mary Carroll

When Tag Hansen's car ran into Lark, she thought it was the end of her holiday . . . until he extended his hospitality and had Lark rearrange all her plans.

Race the Tide by Mia Maxam

Deceiving Scott Kirkner in her mechanics coveralls was fun . . . until Christina fell in love. How could she tell Scott his mechanic was the same beautiful woman he had romanced?

An Adventure In Love by Marilyn Manning

While in London Julie Brewster had agreed to stay with Morgan Stuart, an old friend of her grandfathers'. But Morgan was young and attractive and Julie fell passionately in love!

More Precious Than Pearls
by Susannah Windham

When Manzanillo Arismendi grudgingly offered advertising executive Leeanne Mullins his prestigious account, she knew she could handle it—but handling Manzanillo was altogether another matter.

Silhouette Desire
15-Day Trial Offer

A new romance series that explores contemporary relationships in exciting detail

Six Silhouette Desire romances, free for 15 days!
We'll send you six new Silhouette Desire romances
to look over for 15 days, absolutely free! If you decide
not to keep the books, return them and owe nothing.

Six books a month, free home delivery. If you like
Silhouette Desire romances as much as we think you
will, keep them and return your payment with the
invoice. Then we will send you six new books every
month to preview, just as soon as they are published.
You pay only for the books you decide to keep, and
you never pay postage and handling.

READERS' COMMENTS ON SILHOUETTE ROMANCES:

"I would like to congratulate you on the most wonderful books I've had the pleasure of reading. They are a tremendous joy to those of us who have yet to meet the man of our dreams. From reading your books I quite truly believe that he will some-day appear before me like a prince!"

—L.L.*, Hollandale, MS

"Your books are great, wholesome fiction, always with an upbeat, happy ending. Thank you."

—M.D., Massena, NY

"My boyfriend always teases me about Silhouette Books. He asks me, how's my love life and natu-rally I say terrific, but I tell him that there is always room for a little more romance from Sil-houette."

—F.N., Ontario, Canada

"I would like to sincerely express my gratitude to you and your staff for bringing the pleasure of your publications to my attention. Your books are well written, mature and very contemporary."

—D.D., Staten Island, NY

*names available on request